in the river running

or

choking on water &
white bread

by adrian pedraza

copyright © 2024 adrian pedraza

all rights reserved. no part of this publication may be reproduced, distributed, or transmitted in any form or by any means, including photocopying, recording, or other electronic or mechanical methods, without the prior written permission of the author, except in the case of brief quotations embodied in critical reviews and certain other noncommercial uses permitted by copyright law.

in the river running or choking on water & white bread

dedication

thanksgiving break and those nine days off

dear happy howard, tony toolbox, the rest of ya

it has been a long time. i've been meaning to write. i know youve got some questions and i havent got all the answers yet but im working on it. i got your letter–in case you were wondering–and i read it all the way through–twice–its nice to start getting those again.

the following pages attached to this envelope are a trying start at an explanation of things–rather, the whole lot of everything that transpired in the last year or so. i mean the most important parts–striking parts–jarring parts, i guess–in the last year or so. i think it was all under a month. i remember it like it was two weeks ago, though some of the minute details still slip my mind. now summer is coming and the rain is starting to stall, even though it still gets freezing cold in the nights. must be those snow-tipped mountains up behind the clouds–you know them, im sure you remember them well. have some kind of picture at least. anyway, i found my actions to be somewhat questionable and out-of-character in that time but i dont want you to take this as an apology. take this as a glimpse of my feeling. i am not sorry i had these feelings, im sorry in the way i went about them. and maybe you could learn from them too–not that i am any kind of teacher. just think you outta know my own before ya act on any kind of spontaneous decision like i had and did and still do sometimes. its a piercing, questioning stumble. but before i get any more preachy i would like to let you now the following: this letter took me roughly two days to complete and i threw everything on there–for better or worse, youll find out shortly–and in that wild frenzy (the likes of which i dont even remember most of) my ink ribbon started fading but i had no time to change it–as i was in it–so the last coupla pages might be somewhat faded but you should still be able to make them out, as i remember typing them. also, this is so long because i couldnt make it any shorter. this is just as it is. i had no time to reread or rewrite or see this or that, so if it comes off a little jarring, reread it slower, i guess, or skip over some passages for the point, because im sure everything i learned/you need to know is in there. i was so worried and filled with anxiety in getting and sending this out that i had it sealed and wrapped the night of finishing, and i am penning this letter right now outside the post office (this is why it is taped to the back).

i thought itd do good for an intro instead of throwing you right into it and ignoring your own writing–which, again i got to and through twice. thats all i got for now. i hope you understand and if anything enjoy some of my incoherent ramblings. hope to see you back soon.

with love and feeling,

phoenix

PART ONE: LOST TO THE BEAT OF THE DRUM (& A SMOOCH OF ROAD RASH)

stop, she said faintly. muttered at the end of a struggle of skin and arms and legs and muscle, tense. stop, again. so delicate. you could almost not even hear it. a whimper, a whisper, a moan. it was intriguing. you could just dive right in. i wish i could. but i couldnt. then, fluffy fingers around my wrist, locked and squeezed.

hey, she said, clearer, louder, sterner. stop. wait a minute. stop it for a second.

oh, i looked up through strands of wet hair stinging my eyes and salt across my greasy forehead and i could feel the acne growing and pulsing and hurting and irritating. sorry, i panicked. i didnt mean to. i didnt even realize. im sorry. i wasnt sure.

she looked at me, eyebrow cocked in the dark blue of the dingy backroom dwelling. i could now feel the awkward arch my back was posted up in, and the musty hair-infested carpet had rubbed my knees and elbows a swollen red.

then, maliciously, frustrated, are you good? she said.

what?

are you even up?

i looked down at my briefs. i didnt need to. i knew. then back at her, mouth open, eyes studying hers, freckled and round and nose smudge like a pug and hair flat greasy curls, and lips fire hydrant red and eyeliner by her cheek and nose and smeared and a whole muddy mess a fire. i dont even know what im doing. i thought i was attracted to her. not just in the dark either.

no, i said.

okay.

she rolled me off, pushed down her thrifted gypsy skirt and found her dilapidated mary janes. she waved around her arm until she caught the rusted metal beads hanging in a steady silence and yanked it downward, hard, too hard, unnecessary. the buzzing yellow light and fan twitched on, revealing our shrunken headquarters, its walls pale and peeling, old movie posters and flyers decorating it like show girl make up. all an act. all a gimmick. she huffed and puffed and frustrated and angry actions but instead of giving an explanation and examples of what, she slammed the heavy wood door and left me alone with the short swaying of the fan about to come off its hinges and me not even panting and no sweat broken on the floor looking up at the ugly tweed sofa that housed the rest of my faux attire–from the boots to the jacket–and getting up i slipped on my jeans and found that any advance shouldnt be taken so lightly. and this has never happened before, but theres rarely been anyone else before. and actually there hasnt. no. and this little green room began reeking of piss and wasnt as romantic as i had thought. and is passion real. and who left it by the van and the dumpster and have the rats got to it yet and have the skunks got to it yet and have the raccoons taken it to their temporary sewer homes?

i waded out of that room pulling on my coat, and stumbled right onto the little plank wood stage where i aimed for a place to sit among the heavy crowd–my thirty-second spontaneous date was already lost with the rest of em–and found the holy resting place back by the far end of the basement.

i would have rather been freshly showered–though still in my clothes–i guess it would make more sense if id just come from a lonely swimming pool or water hole. anything but sweat. but it was sweat. and i had to deal with the sweat. and me, sinking into the end of this rotting old lady couch; in which my knees could almost touch my forehead; in which i would be mashed before i reached the concrete roach floor. another basement night–almost–over. i could smell the wood shavings on my knees, fresh and laminated, and almost see the blood on my shirt, hard and black and still. i banged up my knuckles pretty good tonight; not accidently, of course, i was really digging hard for a reaction from anyone or anything. but now im sweaty and alone. ah, the wisdom of post-modern night. one tired climax into the crowd and now the sitting mumbles of pruney old man. the hours can wear on ya–i label myself a cynic.

a couple, or a coupla couples, took over the other end of the couch and shook it violently–this i could see from the swimming of my plastic cup, and its water droplets soon to be forcefully extracted. and all this while i wondered why it couldnt just magically fill up for me again, while i stayed focused on my knees, and very well should have been on them at this time, begging for caffeine. i usually hated the sounds of smacking lips and hard laughter, but thought the organic spasms coming periodically from my left were a bit more digestible, as even i felt under the covers myself just now. i was content on sitting and waiting this out.

i sighed out loud, rolled over by the cafeteria-ruckus, put one leg over the other, and tapped on the faded suede. so many bodies. like ninety-eight-cent goldfish. and the dimmest of all basement lights to allow a few side-eye glances while i conducted my studies.

jacks long, bumpy spine was only a few from my right. his shirt, wrinkled and soaking too, looking like a grand cape draped over him, and his baseball cap replacing a would-be cowl.

i leaned toward him and spoke,

jack. hey, jack...

he was working his way around a mumbled conversation with two coffee-shop-types in order to get back to his friends–or drinks–his red cup was empty–or sounds, or the van, girls if he could find one, girls if he could hook one–though he had THEM backed up against the brick wall, by the looks of it.

jack! i called, fingers cuffed.

he caught it, quick-turn, huh? yeah, whats up?

lets load up, jerking my thumb, and...yknow, split.

what?

he leaned in, then spun to the two fellas, motioning toward me, hold on guys, turning back, what? leave? you ready to leave?

yeah, i nodded. a questioning smile, squint, and preparation for answer.

gotta give it...his hands revolved, head rotated, like 30 more minutes. we drink, get paid, we dip–get tacos. sound good?

sure, nod, but i aint gonna eat, probably.

fine with me, just dont get lost before i come get ya with the money.

raising my empty cup and taking an empty sip, right-e-o.

he got lost with the wave of colorful locals and one of the ladies at the end of the sofa ripped the lips off her new skin and bones and i caught her glance from my peripheral—my sudden disturbance of the cushion mustve upset the mood. i tilted my head her way, almost caught her ugly and condemning eye then leaned back my wet mop before she could shoot me down. then i got all too comfortable.

the next time i opened my eyes some bodies were gone, and although we were still a decently packed can of tuna fish, i had dried off mostly. wrist watch read three-hours-later, and lonely sweat-stained couch read some boys just got lucky. jack blended in with the scarred bricks of the set wall, and it was time to get some air.

cut through the sludge and awkward flirts and climbing the skinny stairs to a crisp, somewhat lively askew nightly street. yellow street lamps stained statue silhouettes against wet concrete and green posts. and shops closed long ago still glowed like little nightlights for the conversationalists that were spread about in comfortable universal purple nowhere.

i stumbled out of the small alleyway, between staircases, and manholes, and book box glass windows galore, and while trying to regain my energy and trying to fully awaken. i shoulda known. i finally took off those stupid gas station sunglasses but they leapt from my fingers, and decided theyd feel better under my boot. i shoulda known. but i was thirsty. still had an eight hour drive ahead of us (if we wanted that seattle show–of course we did–but its gonna be one hell of a drive). the whole atmosphere was caked in cigarette smoke–once the breeze went still–and running my leather hands along my drooping face only grew the madness. i need to stay awake.

some smoking waxed eyebrows and spiked denim pointed me toward a 24-hour diner where they said it would have shit coffee, but good coffee. i thanked them with white frost from my lips, pulling my faux closer, and stumbled off like a drunk to a whiff of barley. but id never had a drink before, so i dont know what i was talking about.

following a steady trail of puddle glares i almost dozed off again, and with my hands in my pockets to keep warm my balance was that of a teetering toddler. when, finally, a pile of floating leaves did not let me pass by so pleasantly and decided to act like a slick of ice which caught my boot sideways and greeted my back just as fast.

id had many dreams before and even use to keep a thick little journal of all the notes and things i could remember. i saw a lot of modern worries and only walked the old rope bridge leading back a few times before. usually them old characters would greet me on my new path and id completely forget about everything and anything and shake their hand. though awkward and sometimes jarring, these mini-movies were more than welcomed, and even got enjoyable when i was able to sleep comfortably– even if just a second. and all these dots came connected whenever i woke up and had a pen and dots to connect, or else faded away into old stories, which, with constant retelling, became more legend than actual happening. all i remembered this night was working in the back of a kitchen with some girl. on what and with whom, i could not tell you. usually im sure if there was more to it or if it had just left me, but this time i was sure i only had that blurry glimpse: back of kitchen; girl; hands busy, both of em. then a large metal something toppled over just out of view–i was looking down at her–a great, wild tumble. metal clangs and bangs and things. i meant to look over, im sure, but i was busy studying that serenity so focused. her head turned, i gasped, something else fell. missed her face. dammit. avoided it. probably.

this time i jolted over on a black asphalt bed and slimey leaf tongue slid down my cheek. then some other pot crashed to the ground and i rolled back trying to ignore it. again. eyes opened quick; starry mute black pulsing sky. again. then some whistles and high-pitched cheers. no kitchenware. my ears twitched and eyes were rubbed like a restless dog, and a lost saxophone some place far off comforted my soaking aches before i realized this was a band. and a thumping bass rose me to my feet like pounding angels. alright. im up. i hacked a cough and dusted myself off, bundled up, trying to warm with a wet jacket. i thought to my vanished dream. i see you. i keep pretty people in my back pocket–on the street, in the shops. only one or two ever by the breast. just one, i guess.

ive got no direction to remember and the map of words given to me was wet on the ground and destroyed with the scattered roars of automobiles passing by. to the music i shall go. then to the music i had went. to finish off the rest of this dragging walk–

id left school sometime ago. on a sharp winter day, just before break. the books and papers and all of that werent so bad, and the teachers were fine. but when the bad days grow worse, and the worse days grow long, you search for a mutt to beat so you can nourish the cat. and professor one, on one wednesday had done nothing wrong, objectively, but something wrong, subjectively. to one itching bone along my body. one i could not yet find, nor scratch, nor hear, or yell, and i left in the middle of lecture with my bag still open and my papers still displayed and my lines still anecdoted. and i was stopped just by the last few empty chairs and questioned, calmly and motherly, hey, is everything alright?

and immediately nodded, i did and turned my head, staying still, but alas there were no second thoughts and i nodded some more, yeah. sure. i just got this thing i really gotta git to right now, and i pointed toward my golden gates of heaven only a few steps away, the slow-moving metal door.

oh, okay then, she smiled with her arms folded and her coffee breath and her stance in that english professor pose, you have a good rest of your day, then. wissfully and mock-obliviously and a little let down. thats for sure. i would be.

i smiled and winked and took off my clubmasters, will do. will do. and i never unbuckled my seat belt that day, and the papers on the desk grew yellow and lost meaning to any scholar, and the years went by, and the road never did, and the highway never narrowed, and i still hadnt found that bone to scratch. but i was moving. and as long as i was moving and the lands blurred in motion, i knew id hit a target somewhere. i just knew it.

well, what the hell do you plan on doing? i was often questioned by my aunt. and i just as often told her, hit the road with the band and make alotta money, or something thereabouts. i had wanted to visit paris too. id never been.

what? she mouthed some more, never quite fully expressed, but her eyes liked to remind me i was insane. how they darted up and down and studied my very serious stone expression. id feel bad about it, this coldness in my perception of reality, but not in the moment. and this was when the seeds of irritation were planted and i hated the noise.

so off i went to put dog food in an empty dog bowl. one that was never touched by an animal. one that still reeked of dog beard. and off i went to fetch her leash that hadnt been around a burley neck in some time. and down my pocket. and out the front door to get my fix. i didnt slam it. i wasnt angry. i just needed some time to myself, then i could come back all smiles–then i could come back and even finish school–once i made enough dough on the road. but as i reached the last step, the door swung open behind me, and a bluejay lost its footing in a spaz and flew away.

and just where the hell do you think youre going, pheonix? that tired question. she knew and i knew. she knew and i knew.

i swung around in a haste, my messenger bag flopping along as i continued backward. that tired answer, im gonna get my fix! i called back with a wave and a smile.

pheonix jackson! where are you going at? that same perplexed, alienating look.

im gonna go get my fix! i wrestled my pocket for a litter of black and clear purple crystals, then raised a handful high to the late morning blue of sky, shouting back by this time so she could hear me, the rocks havent been working! and one final wave and one final spin, and my collection of stones bouncing on the ground, and the coughing ignition, and the car roared to life, and out the driveway with the slam of the front door.

as i reversed, our old neighbor pamathas door creaking and crying awake, shuffling outside in her raggedy pink dress gown sizes too big of her already hefty body, and her look of the devil: that evil nun eye. even though she had no time to be religious, or show she was religious, or anything religious for that matter. as she was too busy all the time fattening up her pussy cat or watching game shows played at crackling volume or slowly dying on pills and medication, and some wild guffaws at the mailman and his short shorts.

waving her cigarette wildly, smoke whipped round like a lasso, she hurried to the edge of the porch as not to miss me, and screeched out her throat, ya bum! yurra bum! yurra bum!

i didnt think i was a bum, in the bum sense that she had meant bum anyway.

half-cocked smile and tired wave and i rolled down my window, not to respond, but to get a taste of the air. and finally get a move on.

but on the deserted street, rustic orange and yellow fall leaves taking up the empty spaces of college beaters and old jalopies all gone home for the holidays, my hand seemingly slipped the car into park–right in from of ol pamathas too. and my hand also seemingly cranked down the passenger side window–which gave a perfect view of ol pamathas too. and my throat seemingly cleared itself, my eyes seemingly locked onto hers, my face seemingly matched her grimace and the air seemingly unmoved like the wild n empty pause of a hand twitch right before a duel. and then, youre god damn right imma bum! and youre a fuckin bum too!– and the madman laughter as my little car chirped up the road and whirred down the street. no more need to drag me down. i never said i was on top of the world. because id always wanted to become it–

inside another dimly lit little venue. except this time a little band of black musicians was on the almost non-existent single-step stage. sharp n snappy drums, stand-up bass, all that jazz–and thats exactly what it was: jazz. i didnt even know they still played jazz, thought it stayed and died in the past.

the sticky wood floor was furnished with great giant sofas and love seats, where upon small coffee tables were placed haphazardly among them. and although the place was crawling with cool cats, i felt warm. the large mahogany counter took up most, if not half, of the entire room, and looked like it could take the whole building with it sliding down the lopsided street. but the crowd of skinny beatniks might have balanced that weight just right. i mean it was crowded more like a bar that sold pastries and lattes rather than bottles or lunch. and would my presence disrupt that weight? perfectly balanced by all these immutable factors? coffee just needed to be in my hands, that was all. and i would be gone in the morning...the morning.

yeah, thanks, a cannoli and small paper cup handed to me over an old glass display of delicacies. and whats the time, do ya know?

the old womens lips stayed tight and still, and curled to a pitiful frown and shrug. she was busy and went to the other end of the counter.

i took a too-quick regretful sip of the molten beans and focused hard on nothing in particular, just the moment of feeling still and somewhat satisfied. the six dollar doughnut vanished from my fingertips in a chomp-and-a-half and my wallets stomach growled.

still feeling fuzzy, i leaned on the wood top and sipped my drink carefully this time. in my overencumbered struggle to remember my dream i hadnt realized thered been a lively murmur beside me. the music seemed to have stopped for a minute or two, and now i could really hear that collective giggling. i decided to bite my tongue, take a deep breath and glance my pupils over. the slim sweatered back of a tiny girl in a blur of room. i aimed to my drink and stirred it around with my other finger, it cooled off some now.

her voice chimed closer, continuing talk but getting nearer, then a small thud, a steady tsunami of black liquid, flash flood of my section of the bar. i didnt move until a frantic,

oh my god, i am so sorry!

i looked over to a ghostly pale cat-like face, features so sharp and minute. a familiar likeness. i thought i knew her. but i didnt know her. not this time.

its fine. frozen.

oh thank god. im so sorry, she broke into a wide-toothed grin, clawing at her high cheek bones to ease a coming laughter.

i stayed still. inspecting, ruminating, observing, and questioning. you remind me of someone. i wanted to say it. but i didnt say it.

hey, i turned over my mind, do ya know the time?

i think its three–

the skinny wood door bashed open, rattling itself back to calmness. the two fellas from earlier walked in, backs straight, faces red, and looking to ease their hunger.

the rounder one, pony tail, glasses, and beard, reached the clerk between us, while his lanky buddy, almost a complete opposite–besides the swaying drunkenness they shared–stood awkwardly behind. and tearing open an envelope, the little man ripped out a wrinkled twenty, only thing open now. i want a doughnut, lady–um–please?

he eyed me over from the side, then recognized me, then turned to face me, then put both monster palms on my shoulders like he was gonna toss me out the window. shaking me slightly, he went, hey, man, youre buddies looking for you back at the bar–cafe–lounge–sorry...the basement thingy.

a wiff of moist bottle breath.

ah, shit, i said, taking a final gulp of coffee, thanks for the tip. but he didnt hear me, he was collecting his pastry, somewhat perplexed, as it was not round with a center hole.

i stumbled out of his grasp and went off outside and down the road back to that place of music vomit. i doubt i would have said anything anyhow—to the girl. though i had much more to say. i think. save it for someone else.

how are ya, huh? you good? jack smacked me sharply across the face, and my elbows raised too late to block it, hands still deep in my pockets. it was his way of being the older brother.

where were you? he continued, inches from my nose in his sudden late-night irritation, ive been looking all over for you. carly said you went for a smoke, went to the bathroom. i was looking all over for you!

im sorry, i said, feeling the weight of the night tied to the back of my skull, you said a few more and i went out for a second and this and that and i dont know who carly is and—

hey, he smacked me again, sharper, harder, swifter—a true father figure—and my arms went up the same way in protest.

wake up, baby, we got loads to do. we gots to go, go, go!

yeah, i said, rubbing my stinging scruffy face, i got that.

too slow for jack, he slapped me again. this time shaking me a short seizure trip, i rubbed my forehead, god, man. would ya quit doing that?

you need to wake up!

god damn, i spat, yeah, i got ya. lets load. lets load.

i almost made it past him, then he slapped an envelope on my chest and i flinched and he motioned for me to grab it. it was already clawed open.

whats this?

pay.

i lifted the single bill to the single yellow bulb of the thinning room.

ten dollars? split?

between the two of us? pay was sixty-forty. but i guess not a lot of people showed up tonight.

ten dollars, i questioned secretary hamilton, theres no way. smelly and his friend got a twenty and some else– they didnt even bother to open up the envelope all the way.

lets load up, he said again, sternly, and ripped the paycheck away.

not a lot of people showed up? i followed at his heels, thats crazy.

great show, a steaming bassist said to us on the way to our gear. another great show, from another musician of another band who wasnt even there when we played, but clapped when we finished, and i dragged through another set. i guess they wanted us to shake hands with our hi-top converse sneakers, blue jeans, and whatever else–bootleg ray bans if i still had em.

how long have you guys been playing?

ten years, i told him.

ten years?

yep. ten years.

ten years! thats amazing! you must have been what? third grade when you started?

i was an infant.

what?

i was born to rock-n-roll.

short glance–almost insulted–then he quickly shifted to jack. if he had kept on talking to me i would have clocked him right across his mustached face. but i didnt. and i wouldnt have anyway–

in the dim early hours of morning jacks van choked on the road. spurred and gurgled like the old dog it was. i never knew much about cars. and still dont. which is why i didnt question him when his dashboard lit up like christmas lights in the fall. and in the middle of the rush to leave the bay there was a quick snap under the hood and an instant loss of control of the vehicle so we rolled to a jarring halt just off the exit.

still and no comment from me as–in an instant rush of anger–jack wrestled with his seat belt and slammed the door a few times to get it shut. lifting up the hood of his baby, pained by years of domestic violence, and murmuring loud vehicle slurs i didnt quite understand.

beater! junkie! no beans! no beans!

echoed sirens cried from under the bridge, as a stampede of engines roared on above, below, and beside us. we were under the bed of a running america, and racing to stranger destinations we all were too, and all were accustomed to. the free newspaper i grabbed rushing out the door of donut debbies–that being the only thing i could afford, and the only thing to keep me from watching jack chew in slow savory satisfaction, distract from my bellies harrowing temper-tantrum and wales–was dated several months back, in the summer. nothing new here anyway, nothing i didnt already know. and in the local scene section were the black and white photos of yesterday taken on the modern equipment of today. and the same fun-sized candy circle jerks were being thrown around by the same fun-sized candy circle jerks that i had met through my abrupt stay in the city. i laugh, but they make me jelous.

the hiring ads were jarring and threw me off instantly from the review so it was banished to the dusty dashboard. i rubbed my hands and shivered, forced myself out into the biting blue–on a clear sunny day, even–and stood by my door, facing the dirt and gravel lot,

need help? i asked.

what? an oil-stained voice called back.

need any help?

no...no, god dammit. we got no—a pause for a hesitant, careful coming-to-terms inspection—we got no belt anymore. god dammit.

deflated. that was the sound of total defeat, coming from jack. his god damned car doesnt work. and i thought god damned belts went around your god damned waist.

unless you got friends in frisco, he continued, slamming the hood, who love to drive...then i guess, in our own right, weve become a coupla locals. he rubbed his cold white, sleeveless shoulders and a puff of white breath from his nostrils, now lets find some shelter. i need a coat and a drink.

i know a place.

yeah, where?

should only be a thirty-ish minute walk from right here. i think.

what is it? a restaurant?

spunky little cafe, i said, and they got more drinks than coffee too. that i didnt actually know, but i knew he wasnt fond of coffee, and i knew i wanted to go back for a secret longing that i always—usually—had after sleeping on a short, uneventful conversation. i needa move on with my life. i think. jack called it my addiction to affliction, and his pretty sounding word-plays were why he was the one on the mic. the one who strummed the chords.

then ill follow your lead, he fixed his brandless baseball cap and wiped his glasses with his shirt, only diluting the already-foggy frames with oil: finger and synthetic–

hunched over, frantic, arms waving around, literally searching for an answer in his movements. all this commotion screaming to view from the muted space of a telephone booth across the street. people, young couples. young suit-wearing, coffee-weilding pacers going to and frow as the sun called on to its people: from orange to yellow. time to wake up.

the cafe, now a calm and steady place for study, definitely felt brand new, untouched. young fair-skinned baristas took complicated orders from the local passerby. and text books and binders took up most of the tables rather than jazz and secondhand smoke. this was its daylight plain sight disguise, during weekdays i guess.

before jack left to call our washington venue, which he was currently informing (or arguing) of our sudden and hopeless problem, i begged him for a buck-fifty, which he reluctantly agreed too, and bought myself a small black coffee, which i slowly enjoyed, sitting at my sticky wooden table. ill have to pay him back. and i will. i will.

the stage seemed awkward in silence and terrible paintings surrounded its soundless walls. the magic found in the moonlight seemed to be a drunkards fever dream in the sun. and their heavy, slow breaths disperse that fog in the air and you realize what youve been smoking was the tailcoat highs of hallucinations and delusions pretty in your pillows and horrid in your work shoes. and now i was stuck in a fake ghetto thinking of conversations with little ladies that played back like broken records. and felt like them too, in the reality of the moment. only to move on. only to get away.

jack came pacing back. i forgot the old tote of drum sticks at the last venue and i didnt have any money.

deed is done, he crashed in and rushed over, now we needa find a way to smoke this joint.

they got soda–

a short black figure, rattling chains and jewelry, had stopped and done a double take right beside the table, are you–are you guys SIREN?

jacks smirk took over his long face. he blinked, turned, and pushing back his glasses, left a dingy black streak of oil across his sweating face. why, yes-we-are.

oh my goodness how lucky, her small shout of excitement like curving wind around your ears, like a lazy popstar. i caught your show last night. it was great, are you guys recording soon?

were booked for janurary, i forced myself in, dont know how thatll turn out, our guys busy doing his own gig, yknow? or, i dont know what the hell well be up to.

sure, sure, she smiled at both of us, well...thanks for stopping by. i got one of your shirts, its super cool, man, thanks.

no problem, jack with a nod raised my coffee, my pleasure.

smile, blink, and a wave, then she vanished into the jazzy jungle. like a little mouse, dressed for the occasion, and striking in her blue eyes–the compliments never did stop feeling good.

jack contiued, i gave dennis a call, darby–they owe me one–said they can come by in a day or so, maybe less, maybe even today, then well steer back on track. hopefully no more phonecalls to no more venues. jesus.

tell him to take his time, i winked, we can hang round here for a minute before we jump back to business.

you beat that kit pretty hard last night, howre the skins holding up?

ah, eyes lowered into that minute sea of coffee, forever churning and burning into a hypnotic dream-like procrastination. both cymbals cracked–

the new ones?

yeah.

damn.

the little toms going, big ones fine, losing snare wires like fucking money.

how much money you got left?

teeth gritted, i spent it–shit, and i lost the last of my sticks back at the basement too.

leaving you with what? what can you ration? cause, member that shits closed the next five days and id rather be outta here by sundown.

nothing.

a leaf crushed from flapping thrifted boots as someone came in from the sidewalk.

what!--looking around to see if hed caused a scene just yet. not yet–what the fuck is wrong with you? he went, a little quieter. you dont even care!

what do you mean? these things just happen, i never did none of that on purpose!

you see that chick? asking us about our shit and wanting more? what else do you see but good omens? youre wrestling in the dirt with yourself, when a golden robe and white gardens lay just off to the side! if ya just turned over, youd fall right into divine hands!

ill make it–well make it–i know what im doing, got a few stressful sips in, youre gonna question my loyalty? when im here, drinking coffee, eight hours away from home? hell i dropped everything for this! couldnt help but smash my fist on the rickety table.

you hear about that guy? jack hid his cards, triston benson, the butter churner? he cut off his legs, just above the knee, did you know that?

who? what?

my buddy, he knew him, he mailed me that newspaper clipping from back home in the east. guess ol benson kept dozing off at this farm he was working on, he was an addict, messed with junk and all that, yknow? he was scared shitless of getting the boot because bossman was hard on him--well, mostly the animals too. guess he saw a lot of yelling and soreness toward the cows and pigs and the like. i dont know. something like that. well benson knew nothing else, all his life hed been a butter churner–story goes his mother taught him in his youth somewhere in the midwest and its what he first found joy in, felt only like an obligation as he grew older. but, sadly, he knew nothing else (thats just the story as it goes, as it was written, but i dont think its no bullshit. not at all). well once he got a bit older, had nothing going on, he got involved with all that bad stuff. junky, they called it. just to keep on the highway, stay on the block and do the whole round trip. and so he felt that hed just do better to saw his legs off with some old tool he found rusted away in the shed, in order to live forever (with no legs i wont feel the need to play or do anything else because ill be built for my one thing, is what he thought, my friend said, the one thing thassa slipping away-way-way, or what he thought he said). so one night, after getting another scolding–first time the bossman actually raised his voice–benson stumbled into the shed fearful of his common distractions (not high, supposedly, either, as the story goes, but completely straight and sober) and sawed off his legs in a bitter silence. now, being handicapped to a chair for the rest of his days he could do nothing. nothing but churn butter–as the story goes–because he had to. because he felt he had to. he had to churn butter. no dancing, fighting, the ol fool thought. drinking and shooting-up too, which you could still do, but he broke free of the curse right after this operation, you see, power of the mind, cold turkey and he was free from all of that, but not totally free of nothing else, no.

    jesus, was he fired?

    of course he was! he was crazy!

    whats he doin now?

    dead. poisoned by that old tool–he did get to churn butter for hisself with his mother as caretaker the last few months–even though he hated it, he was convinced thats all there was to do in life–with no legs and all, he solidified it. but the man is dead now.

so, i dont get it. what are we gonna do?

im just making sure were seeing through the same eyes.

i nodded the most convincing nod i could muster up, jaw clenched. convincing even myself almost. yeah, i said, i dont wanna die–

wanna go see a show? jack said. theres this cute little pop duo playing at BLACKEYS, that smokehouse–tonight SURF RIOTS coming with some guys from japan, well, theyre opening for the guys from japan.

my fingers danced around the rim of my empty cup and amongst themselves, nah, no thanks, think ill wander around the city a bit more, see any more omens i can find. im broke anyhow.

no, cmon, we know these guys, they let us in before.

no, thats okay. not tonight, man–

so down the street i walked with hollow eyes and kicking rocks, chanting mantras so they all bounced off the walls and tumbled down concrete ruins. hands in pockets. i was deathly cold. and moving stiff, almost no movement, small shutters. breath-sucking wind shaped my hair to its liking and day-old grease greased it thick, wavy clumps. all this leech to my skin. teeth grinding down. my teeth grinding down. they wanted blood. i wanted blood. nicking bone and melting organs so they churned like chicken soup and steamed through my belly, my body, my neck, and to the sinuses, bursting sewer pipes and swollen.

i shouldnt be kicking rocks. ive never kicked rocks before. im frozen solid. in a fiery green river moving. no grasshoppers around me. theyve swam along far faster than the last breath i ever took, the last blink i ever blank– frogs hopped around their clover laughing. babies, tadpoles, gone as well: just me and the frogs. what a lonley drift, i thought. i thought. but the drug i longed for, unrealized and unknown. the one abused and used and drilled all my complex feeling and action toward–degrees out the window and counting–smashed through. i stumbled into and out of the hallway. i mustve taken a wrong exit. i mustve taken a wrong exit. i was going straight for hours.

in an old letter to my aunt she thought that perhaps the highway had ended. naturally and definitively. and in some divine twist of fate i was sprung back by the slingshot i was, somehow unknowingly, straining forward with a steady jog. then the rocks burst a window through my soul, a pane, already resting outside an unleased ramshackle hole-in-the-wall, already in giant sharp pieces, but now glitter of rain, the infinite and eternal, always there lounging around and awaiting. this delicate waiting glass.

sneakers stomped on a metal sewer grate, no tread, and slipped til caught traction then in spaghetti-noodle dance, stood stiff like uncooked spaghetti noodle. and hands still in their pockets. of course, by bizarre, twist of fate, i was staring at the wood-painted sign of an acoustic guitar. music written crudely over its fretboard. and hanging in the middle of the salt and pepper buildings that lined the entire strip, like golden idol shining and glowing and angels singing holy songs somewhere in the background probably.

the need to continue my stroll until i found the edge of earth–somewhere behind a cabin in the woods, a shack in the desert, a tent in the arctic–had irked me so. very much so. but i could not ignore the warm will of god. reaching out his divine hand and allowing me back in. reaching for my legs and opening the door and sweeping me off my feet and whispering subtleties in my alphabet soup–no letters required, i was very superstitious–so i acted on this notion. against my will. id get some sticks and get back on the road.

a homeless man was pissing. a frozen beggar was buried in morning ice. and a couple of sweaty, balding men were bumbling amongst each other, muttering strange, meaningless tongues that grew more intense as they studied their yellow fingernails. and all these decorations to the cake that was a metal gate positioned around the whole of the building. i must have not seen it. it blended in well with the dampness of everything else. but morning was already running and my supermarket watch told me so, and so what was the matter?

a pink slip, announcing the closure of this store and the opening of another, taped behind the glass door. it was a coffin, this building. and inside lay the chaotic whirlwind of leftovers. from what i could see through the dark, empty shelving, shag carpet, and stuffy attic smells, probably. but beside the empty counter, amongst the dust and ruckus and shavings and tools, was a poorly painted black pail, with a cardboard flap taped to the front reading demo sticks. and a good handful of them there was too. slapped by the devil and blessed by the angel. guess its up to me to figure out whos fighting who.

i shook the fence. it was skinny. real flimsy but an obstruction nonetheless. all of it held together by a cheap padlock. damn.

you tryin-na get in there, sir? said the once pissing homeless man, gruffly, watching me from the crevice of another abandond buildings front door. behind a blue battered beanie and tired eyes and a most witty smile. i could see orange teeth through his winter beard.

um, yeah?

dont questionnit, are ya tryin-na gettin there, or nawt?

a last squinting peak through the skeleton black bars.

yes i am, i said.

i-can-getcha-in.

can ya?

it is so, yes. yes, indeed, but nawt fo nuttin, he shook his head precisely, nawt fo nuttin, no. no, no indeed, sir. no indeed.

well i got no money. cant even getcha pack-a-smokes if you wanted.

huh, what, why not?

cause i aint old enough.

ah, ah, no, not very good, no, no, sir, his chin went to fingerless gloved knuckles in thousand-eyed thought. then he started undoing his baggy trousers and they fell to his ankles, with the jingle of his belt. old blue plaid boxer briefs.

what? eyes wide, i spoke hesitantly.

i–i needa tuh pleasure meh, yes, yes sir, indeed. i needa tuh pleasure meh, sir, yes i do–get to suckin! get to suckin! get to suckin!

his screams echoed through the cars flipped upside down, the heaps of trash smoldering by dumpsters opened and ransacked, and scurrying heavy rats and mice with needles in their little rotting teeth. i noticed it all now. ear piercing he made me flinch and so sudden like a door slam.

oh... there was a definitive pause. old newspapers dragged along and flat cardboard cups bounced around like fighting fish.

well–how do i–again, how can i trust you? how do i know youre not lying to me, making me do your ugly deeds for nothin?

he reached into his old tweed new york city blazer and pulled out a murky red tin. still wrapped in yellowed plastic, i had to lean in closer to see that it read LOCK-PICKING SET in 1950s advertisement style with shocked 1950s housewife portrait off to the side.

does that even work? i asked.

of coursit does, sir. iss brand new, stuffing it back inside its musty hole.

i took one last look in the building. the blue air, the white sky, the morning. dangers lit by longing attitudes and gas leaking and dripping from my head. my exposure to hypocrisy. willingness to jump and learning to keep on running along the way. to take opportunity where it strikes and make your own luck. all these chances coming to fruition at one time. and climaxing in literal seconds. if i just make those few steps forward. although i wasnt too keen on having gray curlys in my teeth, i was just as keen in striving for the future. the devil and his saw may kick back, for there is always a knot in the wood. so i walked forward. heavy and afraid and so tired.

dead eyes, frozen, bulging, and bulbed like statue erected. he mouthed his favorite phrase, pleasure meh, and pointed straight down, stomping his feet and grunting.

and so one knee i fell to, and then two, and a forever blink and slow breath, and short whimper.

huh? what–what wazzat?

gods opening hand turned to a wilting fist of enlightenment, and i with a one-two standing and a one-two dropping. the man fell like the ropes of protest wrapped around his stone structure and pulled with the weight of today. in the midst of his groanings and odd gurgling noises, i jacked him for his tin, shuffling through coins and watches and dry, crumpled tissue. ripping out of his coat, he reached for my forearm but only glanced it with a soft rub as i pulled away. more noises, i couldnt help but freeze and stop and stare a moment longer. he was stuck in a state of waking up, buzzed, and hungover from shock.

the lazy gift set actually worked. though it took a bit of thrashing around and i bent some of the rods and such it came with. but the lock dropped to my feet with the pound of the street and i was in. i rushed open the gate and went for the door. nope, nothing, unmoving, i took a few steps back to the rocks i was kicking and grabbed a handful–i couldnt give up now. this was an open hand! and with an overhand toss, bashed the bottom of the glass door, leaving a spiderweb of white shards. in, out with a bucket full-o-sticks wrapped under my arm. one last look at the moaning, mister pleasure-seeker, a decent pause, this one, then took off like the boulder chasing behind me down farther away from the cafe, and wherever i last saw jack–ultimately back and going, i thought in my wild escapades. look at all that ive done for you, i spoke to someone, to you and me and whoever i recklessly thought wasnt listening–

i was busy staring at the black marker tattoo on my wrist–symbol of a lover, friendship, or whatever it could have been–now fading a transparent blue against my white skin canvas. lonely, and pressing for a moment. gave it a good rub. still there. i didnt mind. i liked it. and i missed her. so very much.

a sharpie pen sat in package with receipt in my pocket. time was coming for a touch up–not no kind of rebirth, but rather a stroke of the flame, a kiss on the cheek, hands slipping down shoulders and so delicate, cold fingers–not for long.

they came in! jack pressed me. we were in a theater. the theater. you had to be there. it was local legend. but not nothing unsurprising for a band our size, except, of course, wed sold it out as headliners.

he pointed to the rows of black and white photos hanging above the stuffy greenroom walls, caked in dust and sweat–a shabby black–but an ancient and mythological one: a temple of the gods. of the small college town buzzing.

do you even know what youre part of, man!? of course i did, hed reminded me the last couple weeks. but i already knew at that time. it was an exciting prospect. sure was. and my heart raced quite the stir. my palms were sweaty. but my mind was loose. my mind was wild.

were part of history, man! he caught my eye shift to the rubbing of my wrist, how dreadful for him. he smacked me, solid, pay-attention smack, nothing too serious. i caught wind, looked up, felt his presence.

i know! i said, sharing his enthusiasm, checking my body language. i know! im excited!

you ready? are you ready? his giddiness blended with his need to keep teaching, mentoring, making sure the pieces were played just right. for him. for me. for him.

youre one damn good drummer, you know that? pat against the shoulder. a damn good drummer. everybody says so.

i knew that. and i was ready. i rubbed my shoulder. a spark of laughter. hitting awkward, dying brush, flint and steel. bursting to toothy grin, been years in the making i guess, and, finally, a giggle. been so long, surprised you havent dropped dead yet.

jack cracked. two hands on me now. slowly picking up laughter like the warming of an old engine. and finally a wild outburst of emotion: crying from joy, crying from release of hard work. but we werent on that stage yet. and he knew that. he grabbed hold of my face like a father a pit-bull, squeezing my chin and cheeks like they were slipping away with the years, the time and the seconds a-ticking.

were really here, you know that? you know that? were really here. merely there–pointing at the black curtain door– and on the track.

a great opening for the beginning of a tour–the beginning tour–a first real tour that wasnt a few little shows a few hours apart for three days. we learned our lesson. we hit the road. we made it by the parking lots, record stores, backyard raves, children parties, and more. wed earned our keep. by now. and this really proved that–to the world. or else the kids in the scene, man. and

in our van a couple hundred copies of the first record–a collection of songs and things and bits of poetry built up from our early days of college and now–pressed by some indie label in LA–who also happened to make this shit happen. they sold out halfway through and we had to buy loose copies anywhere we could in every hipster part of every hipster town that carried stuff like ours. it was an exciting time and the years passed by chasing that moment, the loose bags of hanging skin under our eyes pressed thin with duck tape which came out of pocket and we still held a handful of copies of our last record two years ago, or whenever it was, that sat dusty in plastic wrap and under the covers of our van.

jack has no more fingernails, his tips curled with blood and metal shavings, sleepless he calls out to every passerby, handing them the mysterious neon flyer of anything going on; my finger nails curling to the prints over the ridge, and growing smaller in my morning clothes as i dangle along on my leash, chains, cuffs, whatever you wanna call them– but this, this bucket in my hand, these feet wafting through the sand, the wind song of the mad twisting like the tornado sprint i took across colleges, shopping centers, and two-story malls until i reached the edge of the ocean–where i stared off into the chopping waves and gray haze sky that protected the sun from my beautiful eyes, but also kept my skin soft and true and prime from any of the dangers that would have stabbed me in the back–as the seagull calls a conflicting tune and i close my eyes to listen more intently.

thats right, i plopped to my arse, pail in the sand, rattling with sticks and kicks. thats right, i thought. still in it–

jack was sitting in his dead baby van, legs kicked up on the dash and head deep and eyebrows low in some iggy pop magazine, huge naked portrait of lively old man bright and true on the cover, many more of many others tucked underneath his reclined drivers seat.

i knocked on the window, hey! hey!

it took a second as his head moved deeper into the words, rushing through a paragraph, then he popped up like a gopher.

i raised the black pail, full of old drumsticks, and rattled them away through the window, a smile as wide as venice, and thinking back, i probably looked a little stupid, but i was searching for love, and i found it with this beautiful pile of tools. back on the road we would be in no time. no time at all.

but then afternoon came with a rumble of hunger and faded away to an early dusk. and orange sun through thin clouds calling for the moon to take over–we understood it.

music mags littered the dashboard and carpet bottoms, read and reread to oblivian. and finally jack, in his dramatic fashion, threw down the wrinkled paper on his lap, where the fuck are those guys? they shoulda been here by now! which wasnt true, i dont think.

me, silently, writing a letter on the back of a souvenir postcard i picked up a few cities ago, impulsivly deciding to use it to check in with auntie at home. and in this wavering moment of joy jot down as fast as i could how the search of myself on the road was going: it was going just fine, i wrote. i did not want to mention how recent this finding was, though i knew it had always been there.

jack stared at the empty highway, shuddering from the foreshadowed cold, tapping his feet wildly and frantically. then, in even more of his dramatic fashion, threw his magazine up in the air with shrugging shoulders.

well, what the hell, im hungry, you wanna go eat?

i tried to finish my sentence before answering, my handwriting getting smaller and smaller as i got near off the cardstock. smeared and smudged messy blurbs, im sure she could still make out.

huh? you wanna go eat something?

i got no money, i said quickly. i got fifty cents left from you, and im looking to post this as soon as i can–

well, shit, im not going alone–you can watch me eat?...

period, i put the pen down, looked over, no im alright. i think ill wait around and try to sleep.

he stared at me, eyes lowered a judgemental squint. fine, he went sharply. ill get you some grub, but you owe me...and youre gonna have to learn eventually, anyway.

learn what?

to grow up.

–and so we went and walked back down the city area. trash, where that cafe was, but passed it, and looking for a suitable quick and cheap eat we searched in huffy-puffy silence. jack was careful to step over shards of a broken bottle. nighttime had begun early and it was getting hard to see in the purple shadows. the shine of businesses, closed and new, was the only light to our journey.

so, howd you come about those sticks?

well–hell–its kind of a confusing story. im not even really sure what happened.

huh? whatta ya mean you dont know what happen? you just woke up with them in your arms or what?

well kind of. a sporadic sorta thing, yknow? i woke up and they were kinda just settin there.

a what?–

hey!

–shout from close behind in darkness and mystery and empty streets and echoes like a wild coyote yell, shivers up my spine, and hands too frozen from climate and shock to move. i knew that gruff call, and i couldnt tell who stood far back behind me but could make out the broken figure of the once-pissing homeless man and his ragged beard and beanie. but this time he held some kind of short pipe in his hand, everything black like shadows of past in my lazy eyes. and i knew we had a problem here.

jack squinted, who the hell is that?

me, in cold shock-fear, though disappointment of my feeling, thats the goddamn man who helped me!

he started approaching.

then whised he want your skin?

i dont know–

his stocky figure split into three and soon a small army of angry-horny ruffians were pacing toward our hungry bodies, and i didnt want to, but i needed to. i just felt like it. and jack had already put up his fists to defend his pride and me. so, reluctantly with a blink and a sigh i pushed the hair out of my face and spat on the ground. and so much energy and so many thoughts and a rush of emotions and tears behind my hard-pressed eyes and jaw clenched small headache, teeth aching, and nose stuffy whistling with my cold n short breaths and wrists hurt from negative nutrients and now it was time for the release. the release years in the making.

but before i could raise my fists in protest–purposely in slow motion, of course, to show the world my bitterness toward the situation! (ah shame on me, dull and useless pettiness!)--a heavy metal pipe donked me on the head and i only heard the hollow ring of my skull and its rattle before a white flash took over and when i revived from my flinch in a blink it seemed a few minutes had passed and i was sitting like a tired babe on the floor. and what looked like ninjas in black stealth battled heavy, long thrusts and shoves and scruffs along the sidewalk and street, for my saving, and for my ending, i think. and then i went back to sleep with a steel toe to my ear and slept like a babe for a time i did again. no release. such a tease.

mini shards of sprinkled glass rested softly atop my fuzzy shirt, just now realizing it was inside-out and thats why the tag had been bothering my neck. it was dead cold and my arms were frozen and in such an awkward position blood flow was cut off so they burned like hell and i thought they were broken–but a spider, quarter sized stocky ball of fur crawled up my wrist and landed where a fated sharpie smile had been; my quick reaction, jumping to the side and swatting it away, smashing my fists into the ground before it was able to scatter and hunt for other warm bodies. instant head rush but now my bits were about me again and i shuddered and fell back in a curled ball. i couldnt feel any pain. but i know id struggled through a migraine in some kind of dream i had:

    tired and knees aching and trying to leave out of an office filled with steam and smoke and sweat poured off me like heavy rain. i was called back inside for something, just reaching a metal door. i dont remember why. but knew i had to go. there were two hammers and a pickaxe waiting for me on the bosses desk. heavy caked with dust and dull with rust. i reached for them but my fingers were gone. lifeless stubby nubs. fully healed but broken by the continual use and heavy scarred skin. thick sludge of blood ran through my palms and down my forearms. continually getting shorter and shorter. itd reach my wrists soon, i thought. palms go fast. thatll be an easy one to grind down. i stared at them in silence, and through the chaos beyond me. i dont know where the bossd gone. i heard his keys jingle and the heavy door shut. but i knew people were around me with their own tools, grunting and yelling through the smoke and heavy clinks and clacks of the room in motion. i dont know where the boss went. i think hed been the one to call me back in. i think he had but i dont know. and everyone else had their fingers still. and when i went to leave again there was a chain around my ankle. and the key was around my neck. then i woke up. and i was sore.

i shouldnt be sleeping in blankets of glass. what i thought were the eye boogers of a freshened morning turned out to be the flakey dried blood that had ran down my head and dripped off my nose–the man who hit me flashed before my eyes in a blink and a vision and i rushed to see my waist: belt was still fastened, sure thing, and whatever relief could be mustered passed this confusion that fell before me.

i laid my head back, instantly brought it back up again and tried to look around through the blue fog, resting softly on a single chirping birds morning–two bodies lay stiff on the sidewalk, two black blobs like frozen dirt mounds. one, back perched slightly, was a hefty son of a bitch. and a wild bush of stringy hair covered everything from the neck up so it looked like his guts were spilled out in b-movie spaghetti-like fashion; the other, closer to me and facing the sky–could tell by the architect of his sharp nose and open-mouth sleeping–breathed softly, with white puffs coming from his shadowed corpse. shit. and that was jack.

i scrambled to him and one arm was around his neck, acting as a boney pillow to the cold concrete inches away; the other, a swollen pink balloon that seemed to pulse with his heart beat. he looked so young in the pale light and quite literally hungry, like someone took a scoop out of his body, leaving a disheveled crescent from the end of his ribs to the start of his waist. a dead son, tired and tried.

my greasy punk kid thoughts could not muster up a sane decision at this time but i thought id better get him up, a coat maybe–he was sleeveless, as he always argued to be–and, hell, a doctor, too probably.

hey, jack, its me, get up, jack, hey! i tapped his face with my palm, and he fought to swat it away. drool leaked and passed by dried white streams already flowed.

jack, get up, we gotta go, we gotta get you some help. cmon jack, listen to me, get up. jack? jack?

silence as i stopped for response and finally got a low, humming, half-asleep, ow, beaten and heavy. between drawn-out wheezes and sporadic shutters. throbbing pain aching through his voice, mind, and soul.

jack! jack! i hesitated to shout but i had to. i just had to.

jack! i said again. it echoed with the spotted doves coo too.

huh? what? what? he sprang up to his elbows, huh? whats goin on? im up, im up. then he grimaced and with a little whimper grabbed hold of his fat arm and curled back into his fetal position grunting and cursing.

dammit, get up! i yanked him up and wobbled to my feet as my legs cold-started and my head began to throb again. he hunched over, shivering like a poor dog, and stuttering in strange, childish, naivety.

i know you wanna rest but we gotta go, jack. i took off my coat and offered it around his stiff position, which instantly awoke me to one-hundred-percent mind. and feeling the chill like dagger points dancing up my naked shoulders, i shivered too like i was going to cry. jack started to shuffle along with my better-fit stride, and i began my search for a pay phone.

i got em–i got em all, jack began, softly, they–well one of them–and i pulled back–and he got my glasses–broke them in his fist–knuckles in my teeth–or–and–i mean–

yeah, yeah, sure, you got em good, thank you very much for that, jack. i appreciate it very much.

and–yeah–so–cold.

right.

and suddenly the green sidewalk began a dotted red pattern up the middle, like a thin strand of hair. and it steered snakelike in bigger and bigger drops, then back to tiny bursts of mist and finally a seizureing smell stopped us in our tracks. a light pole held up a stiff, vibrating body, moaning like the cooking of a microwave. he was wrapped up, a mammoth covered in rags–hed given up on his journey to wherever after the whipping hed probably had. and the beating he sure as shit got. and though i didnt want to, felt the obligation to, and so went up–leaving jack standing a few steps behind–and started tugging on his skin-tight wrapping to steal it for myself. then, of course, he froze entirely, glanced over, and his big mitt of a hand gripped my toothpick forearm, and squeezed like hell.

im not who you think i am! i blurted out.

who the hell are–hey, i know you! youre that feller from higgins black eye, he started up, toothless gritting of few yellowed teeth, and caked blood ran along his chin and beard like dark ancient river, frightful, painful look, youre little buddy thought hed get a whoopin out the three of us but we left em for dead–

as he grew taller and more frankenstein-like, i fought for my freedom. i was the mosquito with legs trapped in a spiders web, and i began swatting him, hoping to rid of him like some harmless insect. but his grip grew stronger: fighting the southern crocodile. and jack still back there clueless. and jack still back there dizzy. and jack still back there freezing–i wish there were cops to call and a phone to dial them on.

so i started going at his face, clawing and scratching and fighting a hopeless battle and trying to get any sort of reaction. but he tossed me like a sack of garbage with one tree-stump arm. and i landed against an old wooden fence, banging my head and resparking that dreaded infinite migraine fully. but unlucky for me, i was still awake when i hit the ground. and i took my time getting up, so was promptly kicked in the ribs by that same steel toe that whacked my ear good last night. i vomited a small puddle from the sharp pain and from starvation and dry heaved on my side a second before i caught another good one to my temple. and it fixed my head to the wavy lamp post looking so far away right now.

two elephant-strangling hands gripped my shirt and pulled me to my feet where i got a good whack again across the face before i realized i was staring at the mindless pitiful eyes of the enemy. i went back against the fence, almost dream-like consciousness, and saw another heavy fist coming and yelped and fell to my bum to avoid it; accidently landing my right hand on that young pool of vomit. and before his eyes could refocus on my skinny withered body i scooped up what i could and swatted his face full of yellow puss and as he danced for it off i gave him one big shove and he stumbled backward so i could get my footing.

and when he gave me back that devil stare with the chunky toxic ooze dripping a transparent goop down his neck and beard, i rushed him again, this time to the street, where a speeding city taxi cab caught him by the thighs and his giant body flipped wildly over the yellow car, cracking the windshield, deforming his knees, and finally plopping like a heavy bag of meat–which he was–on the hard, real street, motionless.

the car screeched to a stop some yards away and i ran back to a more alert jack sputtering out more gibberish in shock and pointing and eyes wide and we rushed off together down the sidewalk, silenced by the screeching tires of the cab. that was someone elses problem. we were traveling, telepathically, into the greater unknowns of our futures–the two of us–

i got that man to an er, eventually. the least hospital-looking building in all of the bay, and its blinding white lights welcomed us in like a bitter small dog does: a blunt, instant, and antagonizing reaction. and that was that. jack was left to suffer inside a chaotic waiting room–nothing to read but lots to think–and i needed to decompress and i needed something good and i needed to be alone like i had originally planned. so i stepped through the automatic doors and sat lonely, tired, reeling, on the sidewalk curb. palms fell through my cheeks with the slippery paste of drool and i awoke again with the sun on my neck and my nose in my chest and quick check back and jack was gone and the er still full of irritated people and i still grumbling about my belly and i hungry still. but my headache had mostly subsided so i wandered back to the van and dozed off to the city running beside me and passing me by as i hoped for another breakfast—dreamed of one. and dreamed of nothing at all.

and to my apathetic horror, the passenger side window was smashed to nothing. and the black pail of drum sticks was the only thing missing—out of the entire van: records, tapes, shirts, guitars, every jewel under the sun couldve sat glowing in the back seat but the fucker only took my tools. my tools. and the thought of that really pissed me off. and i realized then—and only then, i guess, studying the sparkling glass sprinkled along the seat and floor straight faced—that i didnt really miss them all that much. and that they couldve disappeared with the wind and the rest of my virginity for all i cared and i still wouldve sat flustered at all the other valuable things they coulda snaked. and thats all i cared.

then jacks friends strolled up in their mom-bought beater, throwing around their short, indifferent comments that they missed him and wished everything had gone all right but really hoped they were still getting the fifty bucks jack promised them. and they made the drive and they stared at me with wide desperate gray sporadic eyes, fidgeting their stringy facial hair and rubbing their heads and arms and talking too fast sometimes, for me at least, to really understand them. i dont remember much of that trip, anyway, it had been such a transient experience the last few days, and i slept most of the drive. i did remember their names though, dennis and darby, but only after the fact. the smaller of the two giants kept calling the driver den or den-den.

i didnt have the money on me, but they would get their money—i assured them—and gave them my address so they reluctantly and passive-aggressively took me back to odessa, where my aunt awaited impatiently for another short return home—short, usually, but always welcome.

PART 2: HOME FOR THE I GUESSES AND I THINKS

i took those rickety rotting steps up to the front door—a different color today, a more vibrant mahogany, than the once vibrant blue, or green, or dark red, or basic white, what have you.

i could already smell the new dogs winter coat, like compost. and the small golden ball of fur greeted me with a lick and a smile, but i paid it no mind, as i knew i had some explaining to do. any second now.

home? a voice echoed from the kitchen, home? home already? again?

i pushed the dog away from my knees and it jumped around and scattered the carpet and almost peed but caught my paying-no-mind, and stopped statue still, in focus.

hold on, i scolded and started my walk towards the smell of roasting meat and commotion of clinking pans.

whos there? the sharp, frantic voice called again.

its me, its me, mimi. youre right, im home.

home already? she turned around with her oven mitts and red-stained apron, reassuring herself.

yes, mimi. home already.

whatd he kick you out?

no, mimi, we had some trouble in frisco and had to cancel the rest of the tour. he wouldnt kick me out.

oh, i know, she dropped her front–and cornbread, still in the tray–and came towards me with a soft tilt and grin. taking my greasy hair in her fingers and pulling back the strands for better inspection.

im just joking–now, lemme see your eyes, she studied closer. i was not really sure what she was looking for: bloodshot? strained pupils? acid paper? there were some swollen bruises and bumps, from boots and pipes, but her boney fingers glided right over them. and they were hidden by my tangled hair.

mhm, you taking drugs?

no, mimi, im not taking drugs.

mhm, okay. are you losing weight?

no, mimi, im eating just fine.

youre a god damned liar.

yeah. youre right, mimi. im broke as a joke. havent et in a bit.

then come, sit down, ive got meat in the croc-pot, rushed to the humble ancient wooden table.

ah, thanks, mimi, that sounds great.

so whats next for you, boy? she asked, ripping a piece of meat for herself to taste-test.

hang around until i leave again, i pulled out the old leash from my back pocket and started fumbling it in my fingertips. ive been so tired recently. i think i need to go down to that tarot reader again, see whats happening. the cards or planets, or some shit thatll change my mind, hopefully.

i think youre just hungry. all that running around has kept you up way past your bedtime–literally–whens the last time you had a full nights sleep?

yeah, sure, i dont know. i got up, impulsivly, passing the new dog, and went upstairs to my messy room. with its dangling posters, faded t-shirts, and little trinkets thrown about every which way, i could finally rest with the dust, alone, unquestioned. i just needed a little reset, i kept telling myself. just a rest. just a reset.

the nostalgic winter evening called back memories of silent watching of the rainy streets as bob dylan records played in the background and i tried to understand the never-ending ramblings of ginsberg.

an orange streetlamp shone through the browned windows and welcomed itself like the sun into my dark, personal, cave. reading glasses sat dusty next to an old journal and by that a can of pens spilled over. paper was everywhere, crumbled, framed, or hidden, and i felt like writing a letter. to whom, her voice caught me by the throat, digging in her fingernails, and yanking me back in time with a relentless grip. but i was able to pull free with opening eyes (though they would forever be comfortable closed). all these things on my mind could get me lost writing them out and lost in a fury of nonsense i could find myself in—every single thought retold until it frazzled out into a bitter mess of rants and longings that every teenage boy has, and every teenage boy gets sick of reading about—even if i wasnt a teenager anymore. so for the moment: nothingness. everything could wait, and everything did until deep into the forbidden night—

i ate a handful of cold meat. and picked at cornbread silently in the dark, on the dark, cold, sticky table. emotionless room with no noise except the hum of a focused, cooling fridge. was i banished? had i sold my soul off too far in the distance to see any real results? have i lost the battle with time and eagerness? have the lords come to rip back their free destiny, which they have wholeheartedly given to me? or have i waited too long doing nothing to realize anything? has it been too long, or has the end rolled on some miles back behind old frisco? all this craziness and i couldnt for the life of me understand why the fridge had one job to know, do, and memorize. why has this object, so meaningless, so important, been gifted with the knowledge of all there is? and why has it used that knowledge for centuries and not waned or wavered and did so its job every day without a single complaint or worry–sure, she breaks down, acts up, runs away, but she is always there, always sure, always pure. the frigerator. what a hack! so easily done, shes laughing in my face as i open and close her squeaky doors extracting the different bits and pieces of supper and sides until satisfied with my frankenstein meal. what are you laughing at? im sure. im in this. im worked–ive been working. i run so hard. i push that boulder up and over the hill! i call to sisyphus and laugh at his struggling face and frozen time, eternal question! ive realized my rock! ive got the horses pull, wings, and help to lift mine! im sure! i put them there! i walked up that hill, ive asked the paper cards of psychic widows and they all agreed! im sure, im sure, im sure! fix me a supper and ill be fixin to tell ya: just wait, wait til i get my shot! wait til i make you supper and tell you of all my all-knowingness! just you wait! im sure! im sure! im sure!

and then water leaked from under the big white ice box and when i checked the freezer for dessert, everything was frozen over an inch thick, and morphed into one gigantic blob mess, like a sudden blizzard had swept the west. but it couldnt have been sudden. it was so thick it mustve been building up for years. unassuming–

A POSTCARD CAME THE NEXT MORNING. FROM JACK, FROM HIS HOME–THE COLLEGE TOWN WE MET, WHEREVER IT WAS, YEARS BACK, AND STARTED–TELLING ME OF HIS FURTHER ADVENTURES IN ONLY FEW RESTLESS LINES:

BUMMED A CIGARETTE OFF A PATIENT AND SMOKED IT IN THE WAITING ROOM, HALF-ASLEEP

THEN THEY CALLED ME AN HOUR, OR FOUR LATER

AND THE NEXT TIME I SNEEZED I FOUND MYSELF ON A BUS, THICK WHITE CAST AROUND MY ENTIRE LEFT ARM, DRUGGED UP AND HEADED HOME–CANT STRUM BUT GOT SOME WORDS WRITTEN–CALL YOU SOON AS I GOT SOMETHING GOING–RATHER TELL YOU IN THE MOMENT, I HATE WAITING FOR MAIL TO ARRIVE–HAVENT HEARD FROM YA, WHERE YA BEEN? I NEED TO KNOW.

P.S THEY FOUND TEETH IN MY KNUCKLES AND I LAUGHED LIKE AN ASS

P.P.S DONT WORRY ABOUT ME N ALL THAT BLOOD! NOT ALL OF IT WAS MINE! ILL SEE YOU SOON!

~JACK

a grainy scenic picture of one of the great green lakes of said hometown–i forget its name–was the face of the card and sat pinned above my desk right in the center as to keep me focused. it was shadowed by my lamp.

though the day had burned half-way through afternoon, id kept the blinds closed to keep my privacy from the sun (real sun this time). i had a stack of old writing paper from college days and my head was buzzing with numb ideas– and it hurt a bit–so i found it was only the perfect time to write some god damned letters. to someone else, to anyone at all. and that solid day turned into transitional night time and i had me a mini-novel hand-penned by the time it was time to eat. no one to send it to, no, but the moon, who was just about to stop by for a visit–eventually i wanted to go out and burn it all, over red candle light, without any second thoughts of rereading, but as of now the book sat neatly stacked in front of me. wrinkled, messy, and filled with inky finger prints.

and as all these thoughts came of what to do and who to think about, a little envelope slipped under my door, and the delicate footsteps of middle-aged loafers snuck away down the stairs. a letter–for me? now? that i was only home two days? one crazy coincidence. made me believe it was not sent but rather penned by mimi and perhaps, in a way non-threatening, trying to get me out of the room. but, alas, the envelope read SALLY PRIMROSE, like i knew it would. i marked this day on my calendar, the day of mail, the day of letters. and realized the true reasoning behind my own spontaneous writing, whether i liked it or not, thought hard or improvised, wanted it or cared: i had longed for answers, from people, and from things out of my control...i think this book was going toward sallys way, no matter how much i tried to ignore it. it was, anyway. i still planned to make ashes for the garden. and i eventually did.

i never knew how selfish and childish jealousy could affect me but the beautiful penmanship of her letter, the words so flawless and meticulously crafted, fluttered my wanderlust heart. and this continued until i merely had a heart attack and the words, being mouthed as i went along, flew wildly, spinning across the room, and dancing against the wooden floor as they landed. but that was just the feeling i got from the idea, the thought, and the beauty of a handwritten letter. the real letter, which im not gonna bother with transcribing now (it would fill a good deal of pages that i need to write. and i would send it with this one, but thatd be a waste of time, and im on a roll) asked me the usual catch-up questions: hows the band, hows mimi, and how are you? things i wanted to answer more adequately in person. but the return address still read WASHINGTON and my wrist was still naked and white, missing her most recent mark that sharpied smile. fading in mere days but staining my soul and i could go on and on and on. i had to put the letter down a second, move my book onto a pile of others written but never sent–god knows why. and place sallys next to more from her on my right side, unanswered. i hadnt even told her my dog died, everything was resting so comfortably in the back of my mind. but now i am here.

although i didnt finish my reading, i grabbed an old yellowed flier and began on the back of it,

i know its been years but i still want...

then i stopped and rolled my eyes and sat back on my squeaky chair. blinked twice, long sigh, and reached again for her writing. her next line read,

i know its been years but i still want–

then i stopped again and went downstairs to eat.

mimi caught my brooding as she leaned up against a freshly painted post, an angelic flutter in her eyes and tone.

more words from your forbidden love?

augh, yknow, and i spun around the corner and robbed the fridge of its sweets.

youre the one who called it that before, you know? forbidden love. she followed me, softly speaking, why dont you go for a walk this evening–after you eat–it might help, you havent done that in a while.

yeah, maybe. i stuffed my face with pie, but everytime i go for a walk i almost lose my head.

what do you mean by that?

in frisco–the weather–the locals–yknow, yknow.

yeah…she said. but why dont you just think about it? please? for me?

i will, mimi, dont you worry. you know i will.

did you read the letter?

not all of it.

its weeks old. you ever thought of responding to any of those? did you respond to the last one?

um…i thought i was slick by thinking hard but we both saw through it. no, no, i dont think so–i might have? ill think about it mimi, i will. so i passed the golden dog again with a slice and a half of pie in my gut and another on a paper plate, heading upstairs for the dungeon where i could hibernate for four seasons and awake in the morning.

but halfway through this hibernation, at around four in the morning i awoke, with no real reasoning–i hadnt the need to pee or anything like that. the moon struck the blinds like a spotlight and lit up my room an oceanic blue.

i heard a figurine fall off my desk—heavy and sharp and hard and tinny. thinking it mustve been my little civil war general grant. then again, a following topple, focused, and swift, the general lee, bouncing to rest on the floor beside. one was atop a horse—i dont remember which.

it was like a yin following its yang—maybe the other way around, or hell, maybe i was wrong altogether. but after that, nothing. silence. i was up and my mind was already racing. it caught traction on one loose string and circled back to the morning, then, eventually, the rest of the day: what had i done in all that time? what was my time spent doing? i sniffled from the chill. nothing. suddenly i felt this waking up was an urge to get the train back on the tracks and rush the coal into the engine, for it had been away far too long—

i told my friends i would never drink and so i never touched a drink. i claimed i was never bothered to indulge—but really i just needed to stay in my right mind, stay alert, and stay ready to get back to business. around the same time i had that prohibition epiphany, i had opened a fortune cookie while vacationing in LA: luck is when preparation meets opportunity. so i vowed to always stay prepared.

and with that—and the empty drag of days that had strung along behind me—i felt as if id been lifted out of bed by this past version of myself (or maybe a future successful version, already revived by old ambitions, and forcing me back on the trail before i was too comfortable in my cotton sheets, settling down before i ever reached my silk ones), and gently eased along to the garage where i could get back to it. and now i was alert. and now the hand behind my back didnt feel so gentle, and so i shot up, with dusty drums of black and blue in mind, and started for the door, where a sudden head rush took over me and i fainted inches from the nob. eyes wide open–

in the morning, the same angels lifted me up again, and with a spinning, swaying mind, i wandered down the stairs aided by soft window light and into the cluttered garage where a black kit sat restlessly awaiting its master.

i am here. i am ready to play you. lets get it on.

so it was around seven in the morning when i grabbed a pair of sticks and beat the snare, then the crash, then the kick, and then went into a wild fury for about thirty seconds. and before any neighbors could bang the door and yell at me, i dropped them to the sawdust floor and sat still, the buzzing of calming cymbals fading away with the buzzing of my left ear. sweat did not drip and blood was not spewn and my calluses stayed sealed and full. and this single group of factors infuriated me so–

when i took off down the road, old flyers from local gigs burned like bonfires around their telephone pole homes and screamed with pointed fingers at my feeble knees, struggling to awake. hands deep in my pockets, i dug for myself, something or other, hidden away. i started tearing down all punk posters, jazz gigs, and pop duos for hire i saw and graffitied over the graffiti with spit and nail polish. cigarette butts and beer cans littered the outsides of downtown venues–some shorter boys were vomiting outside bars in gutter drains and squeaking curses to the moon. what was i missing?

i scraped gum off my shoe by the homemade ice cream store as glowing cars passed me in the deep blue of morning–everything was closed for another few hours or so, and i screamed into buzzing bushes where bluejays escaped to the roofs of old brick hotels. and i found myself with a nest of crows outside the courthouse, smelling the green fountain that acted like a bath to so many critters: addicts, squirrels, and the like. my head wanted to fall into my knees but my neck was stiff and i stared red eyed at the rumbling street as more oil-leaking jalopies drove by and rigs began the homestretch to their respective truck stop homes. waiting. waiting. always waiting. and what for? my hammer! i checked my tool belt, and it hung, delicately and beautifully so, it hung like i was on the navy boat cast out to the forever sea, living eternity, and she, with her white gown, flowing softly, and carmel voice, whispers fears of a future widow-hood to the broken breeze away. and i want to climb back down, and swim to her at the evening docks and caress her fine metal curves so. and grab hold of her and pull her close and use her good, but my feet, they were glued to the floor. a chain was tied around my neck and my hands were pinned behind my back. hey, who is that? let me go! let me go! and her silhouette slowly fades with the rolling waves until a white dot escapes with the wind like a cloud of dust and small green night bugs replace her view and dance around a fluttering, swaying light. but my hammer, gone, hanging, still, on my belt loop. hands fazed through everytime i reached to swipe it from its resting. and when convinced i didnt need it, using my knuckles instead–for the time being, at least–i ended up with bone crumbs on my shoes and i could not grip any warm mug or pen or pencil and live out fulfilling lively days alone. it was no use! id drop dead in the middle of the race, and for what!? for what! for what! for what! it irks me so, it irked me so, it is the forever irk, and i cant keep kicking rocks down sidewalks because im traveling further and further from that headquarters i so liberally call my home. and convinced all my friends and family it was my home and wrote and prayed to god about my home and wished upon a star once, twice, every day of my life my home, my home, my home! and oh! oh! when has the grim reaper come? why has his sickle held to my neck and hung around my babys and took her with a wink and a giggle and my hands were freed of the warm weight of significance! and i cried her name forever and ever but there was no echo, and no one called back to me, except all those shadows i couldnt quite hear. but my baby gone with father death and i had no wind at my shirt and was stuck on that navy boat and wanted to cry so bad. i wanted to cry so bad.

when the whiskey-breath of harmonica screamed out from its tinny box somewhere outside the dark streets i fell back on the pavement to stare at the sky. and saw all the dots fading with the running sun and a breeze passed right above me and i stayed stiff. congestion, all up in my sinuses, i could not breathe. and that was why. and a bell tolled eight-am, and everyone woke up and took showers and got suited and tied and wrote their books and ate and rushed off to work and i stayed on the cold plate sidewalk and looked up at the pale sky, with its freckles hiding away with fear and anxiety. but how could a sky as big as you get shy with me, way down here, on this cold plate sidewalk? i mean, can you see me? and one star stayed–a great big white one, blazing alive like cartoon tooth–seemingly to answer my unanswerable question, and hung around lazily in deep thought...

so?

and so a horn honked and she hid away for the rest of the day. and i was left with a blank white canvas. it was an object i knew well, and one i only made myself struggle to understand–maybe i didnt know–but i left it blank because i had to and my pupils slid along its clear surface, studying, watching, wanting. then the question poised to me came from a bicyclist who was riding by in neon and blinking red lights, a tie dye peace symbol on his back with the proclamation, WANTING WHAT? in swirling underwater letters.

a star or two i thought, and moved my hand up as if i was placing them like decorations on a christmas cookie. and i couldnt stop placing fake white dots upon my canvas but nothing was happening and nothing changed. it got more intense, more frantic, and i was throwing piles and piles of green and red sprinkles and layering it with litters of fondant but it stayed a bland, white cookie!–come on! come on!–i ran up and kicked dirt into the air and black rocks rained up into the sky and spurted like geysers and mini war explosions of street gunk. but just as soon as it stayed, floating in the air, filling my sky, painting my canvas, it just as quickly fell back into chaotic mountains and piles of–in the end–absolutely nothing–hey! hey!–so i grabbed it with my own soft hands and tossed it like a quarterback and the dirt grew under my fingernails and my hands were brown, caked with city dirt and rot and needles. needles, yes, i found all the used up needles along the gutters of downtown and threw them into the sky, where they stuck like darts and stayed a while, but turned the other way with the weight of a metal tip and i began running like i was avoiding roman arrows and poisoned darts.

under the cardboard flap of a makeshift house i made a battle plan with the sticks and leaves closest to me, trying not to disturb my new neighbor from his loud and stinky slumber.

little men were branches, everything else a browning leaf. but they all ended up looking so angry–the pawns to my battle plan–and this strategy began to show some stress cracks and i had to give up halfway through because it was over before it even started, man, yeah, damn! it got scrambled by mania of hand movements and i jumped from that old house, seeing all the needles stuck on top of it, and the man stayed asleep.

i wanted to steal something or fight someone, but i saw a lot of absolutely shredded bald men and scary looking night watchmen and decided against it. a problem to fix, assuredly, but i found that kicking invincible bricks seemed to work out fine–until i found out they were not invincible and they started crumbling and falling apart and my shoe began to tear apart and my toes hurt and my toenails hurt.

so just as i was coming to terms with using my fists– once my feet inevitably gave way–i heard a familiar, soft voice–and the hum of a city bus racing off across the country–not just soft but a slice of the ocean soft, a fat stream heavy after rain soft, melted caramel along the edges of a white apron, soft like the bite of a marshmallow, flowing through the cracks of clenched teeth, soft, and so sweet, and wholly my own–if just for the moment. dazzling rainforest waterfall pouring over my little mountain hermit cave, and sprinkles of its magical mist comforting my red hot face and cooling down my britches from their restless tie-up. and her words, seemingly scolding, seemingly questioning, seemingly holy and innocent, asking, patiently, metaphorically, and intuitively,

phoenix? what are you doing?

and i found myself focused on the palms of my hands, seconds away from clenched fists. and they went to my hair, clasping like wild polar bear claws malfunctioning and piqued. and as i started to tear i let go and stood for a minute. my toes really hurt.

me? i said.

yes, phoenix, YOU! what are YOU doing?

–making–plans.

making plans? how?

figuring–it out?

are you asking me or telling me?

i turned to face her, slowly and robotic. and there she was: sally. forbidden love sally, unsent letter sally, unread letter sally, young and passionate sally, beat by the road sally, and made by the road sally. sweet sally, here and there, and gone again. singing on my fence post and painting on my walls. goods baked and hearts taken. the sweet smelling and hair pulling, the lively and innocent, marked and unmarked, fought, and forgiven, shot and unlived, back from the wet and going again. sally. oh sweet sally where have i gone? and what have we become? the months are so long, sally. and you dont need to hear it, because you already know it. and you dont need my help because you know you can help yourself. and i forgot what i needed. and every once in a while i think i figured it out. and i only let you watch. because i keep my eyes closed. and because i try to keep you in my breast pocket, unbothered and unbeknownst to the fact that you could not breathe. you lived in a melodic memory, my dear sally.

your bite still stings, i said–and you sang so softly–in case you were wondering, i said–

and now–like a corgi barking a threat–i thought id fallen even deeper.

but im not biting...im wondering. im curious, what are you doing?

she put down an aged leather suitcase and took off a dark ivy cap. like the bursting of a dam her hair fell out, flowing down in thick long strands.

last time id talked to sally mustve been going on several years now. two-three? damn. and it was a car ride—yeah—a car ride. i know it. an evening where we were racing off to the third or fourth show at jack and is residency at the WAKE UP TO BLUES music club or the WAKE UP everyone called it. a horribly run staple in jacks hometown. and we gave a hundred percent every night, even when management wasnt too keen on doing the same (a whole different story on our uneven wages and shotty pay—i outta tell you about it later).

anyway, this song was playing on the radio—on our car ride—and i loved it so much and i played it all the time and i went out and bought the single and played it at home and even when the single came out played it in the car when it wasnt on the radio. i remember it well because i remember singing it to band rehearsal every night. and singing it out of band rehearsal every morning. and the struggles with sleep i had. and my coffee intake getting bigger and my shirt size getting smaller. i sweated off caffeine and sweated off baby cheeks. and some bags weighed my face down. and i remember staring at my shoes as i walked along looking for another job, humming. and replacing my laces with leather and the tread from my soles turning smooth like a cow lick. that eventually knocked over potted plants for the wind, and carried that soil to the floor of the porch, and the owners of the studio were mad but we never cleaned up that dirt and i let whatever seeds wanted to sprout fall through the cracks and make weeds under the building. and the weeds would hook around my ankles as i carried bags of equipment to and fro that heavy front door whispering the melody to that song and whispering loose barking dogs and colorful sirens a few blocks down. and this continued til the green reached my socks and i left my coat hanging on a chair inside. i stood at the front door freezing and groaning and stomping the floor in preparation for the next few hours id be stuck without an option. it was just what we did.

today, though, i lucked out and it was on the radio–though censored because of course it was–and i cranked it almost to full volume, and i knew this because, though my eyes were still on the road, my mirrors began to shake, twist, and contort and window rolled down to fix them as we went along–and my chest pumped. the thing was buzzing like a crazy freight train as it barreled down the highway, until finally, right before the second verse i heard that feathered voice of hers roll smoothly off beside me.

can i choose the next song?

but whadda ya mean baby were only a few minutes away, if you choose a song then i will have to sacrifice mine, and i really want to hear my song.

i know, i know, its just that you play this song everywhere, all the time, all day, everyday, and, well, i just wanna give the radio a try too. thats all.

maybe on a longer drive, baby, but lets finish this song, first, before we do any more thinking and what have you.

but i dont really like this song–anymore, anyway–and thats why im not singing along. its because this song has passed me by like a flock of burning geese and its all gone.

and that hurt me, for some reason–hell that was my song. my heart burned with possessions all the time, lost or forgotten–so much that particular day that i couldnt believe what i was hearing. my song? my favorite song? you dont like my favorite song? have you even listened to it? i just wanted to hear it one more time, one more time, is that all that bad? so in this fury of passive rage i turned to her and spoke, free and rolling off the tongue,

i–dont–give–a–FUCK.

and those words, replaying in my mind today, left behind the dreaming boy that i so long to chase tumbling along. something was over and i couldnt quite put my tongue on it–innocence? naivety? i wonder–it wasnt the relationship at the time–and i dont know why i struggle with this–but it was something i know it was. i know it was to this day. something ended, something was lost, something shifted as we scurried along. but it wasnt a breaking point. no it wasnt–that didnt happen until much later when she left in a haze and had a baby and i left in a haze and dropped out of my life: the only sensible solutions for control–but a bridge collapsed just outside the bay, no more cars, no more tour buses, bike rides, or people. the ocean swallowed up my pride and everything else and a whole new wave of silence swept through the beaches and mountains closest. if a person had died i couldnt hear their call until much later, an echo as they fell from the thirteenth story–and live with this meditation i do every day and did every day. back when that sharpied smile was still fresh on my mind, ink, and pen. when it was as vibrant as the execution of those cruel words. and when walking wasnt this damn hard.

i looked down upon my blank white canvas wrist today and rubbed it sheepishly.

i was out, i confessed. looking for...my right mind, or left brain, or, i dont know. something interesting, cool, or half-poetic.

she asked pitifully, what have you done to your shoes?

i looked down at them, caked with red dust from bricks and the soles peeling from the suede, and the rubber cracked and stained with black road, shit...i dont know.

well, she said, i know of a good thrifty place down by the university a few blocks away. wanna go getcha some new shoes?

um, it felt like i had just awoken from a long afternoon nap, but the reality was i was just falling asleep again, everything hard to digest. i finally answered, sure.

we started off. me tottering along beside her, carrying her brick bag and breathing sharp misty air. for a while it was silent except for the surviving city animals that cawed and barked and squeaked awkwardly to our footsteps. everyone awake! everyone awake! but the world was still blue and overnight lights still lit up unopened restaurants like torches sparked off in the western night.

whats the luck, she said. nothing open yet!

i shuddered, the adrenaline of my playing and running and digging erupting into the air with a cold sweat and unbearable itch that spilled over my skin like a thick pasty lotion.

yeah, i said. then a few steps later i got the gall to ask, hey, what are you doin back from uni?

what do you mean, phee? its near on thanksgiving. its break time.

oh, but you–or i never–i thought you stayed up in washington during the holidays?

oh, well, i felt like coming back home this time. thats all.

thats good, i said.

we crossed the street to the closed thrift store she had spoken about and it looked like i was getting no new shoes this weekend. but that was alright. we sat on the curb in front of the entrance together under a warm, humming quiet. the fog was so thick i couldnt see the decrepit penny arcade in front of me, but the skies pressuring and endless mouth was still opened and still smiling a teasing smile over the top of us. yes it was. and no teeth appeared or reappeared or said a word. just observed.

you wanna give me another tattoo? i asked low and firm, searching my pockets for a sharpie. and a silence washed over the animals.

um, no, not really, phee. i dont really feel like doing much of that right now.

yeah, okay–hows your kid now?

hes good. hes great, actually. turning three this year–its all in those letters id sent.

ah, i see. havent got to reading those yet. been so busy.

thats okay. i didnt expect you to read them, anyway. i just needed to–send them out. get them out there.

oh, yeah? whys that?

i dont know, she picked up some loose asphalt and thicked it into the heavy white clouds of fog that laid along the street, where it swallowed them whole and made no noise.

something was just itching me too, i guess, she said. i dont know.

mmm, i followed, throwing my own rocks. ive tried writing too. to no one and nothing i think. and i think ill send them out to somewhere on some day to someone too. maybe.

really? can i read them before? or are they meant for me or–?

no. no, i dont know, they might not leave my desk, even–get them shredded at the office or something.

ah, well, nevermind. picking up another black rock, i never get to read your stuff and i guess i didnt really want to today…i rarely missed a show, you know. do you not trust my judgment?

your judgment? what? no, no, not at all, i love you– or–its just, i dont know, you just cant–you just cant read em, im sorry.

she went silent. no whining or complaining. just silent and thinking. maybe about my slip up.

i didnt come here to read them, anyway, she said.

i coughed into my sleeve and it shook an idea into my head, you–um or–hows–hows rich?

rich, oh hes good, hes fine. hes–hes been going through it lately.

through it? how you mean?

well, you know.

and then she took me on one long gone psychedelic journey through the last six or seven months or so. starting with this:

he had come home late one evening from work doing something, something interesting, as hed always said he did. sally used to question his opaqueness but the more often his lateness occurred the more often she realized she would just have to rush home from her job, kick out the sitter, and raise the damn baby herself–things were unfolding in a strange new way and no one knew what they were doing. thats how it is. thats how it was. they were young, they are young, were all young. hell i still got an teenagers brain. youth is the almighty and valid excuse for those who know it. but sally had to keep composure and so, to also keep that comfortable peace, she never spoke out, only asked, diligently and curiously whenever she could–but that too began to waver. and then her black cat became her closest friend and listener–lover if only–as well as tool for escaping those bitter unknown nights. well what was rich doing on these late evenings? these dark lonely nights when he should have been home before supper. he used to pick up pizza if he was running late, she told me, or flowers, or cake, or something from whatever was open in those dead later hours of evening–and they were brushing off the summer too so it began to rain heavily and consistently and no put up and it ran down her face as she closed her eyes and tightened her lips and wished to be asleep and hoped for a few weeks off before she could re enter earth and her city and her apartments and her room and start wearing ball gowns again to spring dinners and wonderful church events. where she could whistle softly with the wind instead of against it and sing back to the birds instead of fight with the crows and drink those fruity party drinks she used to make and used to love so much. where the potholes in the road did not sink deeper and deeper and become forever and forever but instead stayed warm and soft and malleable like the beaches and the sand and the sea. where the waves could cool you off in an instant and the crustaceans could collect your things and keep them safe and dry for your parting and the bed of white fluffy clouds weeped only through the shade and you were always oblivious to the storm chaser's tide that was obviously here and coming. where their gigantic shadows of mass could never reach you or your orange eyelids with your eyes always closed and your head always tilted. and sometimes never did–but this is just how it got in washington you see? this is just how she got in washington, anyway. and i remembered i had been there once. and i thought it was lovely, at the time.

and finally it was four in the morning and raining like hell on one of those endless work days from one of those nothing business weeks in the dead of another one of those uneventful months. and she, sally, had put the babe to sleep hours ago and sat in her favorite blue velvet lounge chair smoking with a book at first but as her red candle began to fade and the words began to blur, the writing fell from her stiff hands, and she stared at the fluttering orange wall in solemn indifference, so that soon she was alone with the rain, her headache, and an invisible cloud of tobacco smoke.

in comes rich, bumbling, stumbling, stubble, and drunk–like he was drunk. he was not intoxicated. by no booze that is–and she wondered where this man had come from. who pulled this hobo off the streets and forced him into richs beautiful young skin and told him, hey, you there, yeah you, go have a baby with that fair lady, yeah you, go do it, cmon, go on, git, go raise a family you have to! or else you will die! and no one really wants to die in reality. so this mysterious hobo stranger found himself a man with a girl, by order of the devil or the devils friend or whoever, and stole his body like the cheeky trickster he is. it was a ruthless thought. and it almost killed her as an open observation.

then rich turned around, smelling unslept, unemployed, and uncared for, and dropped his leather suitcase hard on the carpet–causing a bang and a shout from the muffled downstairs tenets–and he locked the door, shuddering quite loudly like hed just saw buddha right there crossing the street with a joint and a mushroom or a picket sign telling you the way. like something just someone right or someone just proved something wrong. like someone was smoking in the living room.

and so, she, sally, still young in sense and still ripe with innocence, though it was hours into early morning, spoke in her velvet beat red tongue,

so, rich, honey where have you been? what have you been doing? i fear for you, my darling, and im scared you are hiding something serious from me. whats going on my sweet darling?

and he yelped at the sound of her voice caressing his cold wet back and neck like a hissing hot shower stream, and shivered as he slicked back his receding matte brown hair. he rubbed his itchy stubble and stared at the shadow chair with the shadow woman who sounded much like his dear wife and said nothing and felt nothing as though it seemed the apparent flesh and blood was not even there.

and there was no soul of significance that was traveling or racing through air, time, or mind in the free and joyous spiritual act of breathing. but eventually,

you know, doll, i dont gotta tell ya. i know you can hear me when i speak.

but what? what do you mean by that? what do you mean by that, my darling, you havent said a word to me and havent said a word to me in ages, or in three days, or in our youth. and i can't hear you. and i fear for our free times running around the shopping malls and stealing open house food platters and prancing around the garden, even. baby–what is the matter? where have those days gone? and are they gone? and are they gone for good, baby? tell me! oh tell me! oh, please, rich, my baby! tell me! oh please!

and so rich, vigorously scratching his head like a dog and rubbing both sleeves of his coat across his mouth and twisting his broken neck so stiffly and awkwardly, feeling the heat and the pressure of the four walls and shopping lists and the rent and the butter and the cake, cracked his jaw and finally said

but i have been speaking to ya. i have i have i have, even when im not talking and just going, going, going, and living, living, living, you got it, im speaking, you have to just listen! open your mind and listen i can hear ya, you dont trust me, you hate me, you think im a fool. you dont believe me when i tell ya i know, i found, i can see, and i talk to you freely and openly and found god within my heart beating and lungs and god exists he exists he exists, hes in here– he dug his finger into his temple, drilling it in, turning the skin pale, white and solid, then jerked it away with gritted teeth–hes there, you just have to see, you just have to believe me. ive been telling you, sally, young doll, i know, i know, i know, you know! you know! then he let out an angsty growl like a mole was digging deep down into his stomach, deeper, deeper, deeper, while everyone watched with mouths shut and arms down and laughing in their fixated minds, and heads turning away to their nine-to-fives and street designs and moving the concrete country away from the state and the city and the town and the world with cheap hairy rope clenched between the harrows of tough and tired teeth. and he curled into a ball down to his knees, reeling, reeling, like the holy spirit demon of living undiscovered and out of grasp was ripping itself–right there–through his fragile fragmented body, and the twigs he excused for limbs trembled and he could not stop groaning and yelling and giving and weighing apologies. pain and the unanswered and the unknown and the undefinable like chains around his wrists and ankles dragging him down–down–down–down–down–down into the winding leaves of another mother earth, the hard-packed dirt and soil and the dead fried earthworms on the sidewalk, with mountain fixtures that were here, there, undiscovered, concealed, and unanswerable. the world and the weight and the clock ticking. and the fuse losing length.

oh, darling, rich, are you okay? sally reached out from her chair and swallowed the rest of her butt and ashes. but he just kept groaning and moaning and sounding like a loose cannon and probably was just in that moment. and there was no grip for anyone to latch onto. and so before he could fire the ending shots that would lose and ruin his life forever, that scarred his wrists and thighs and cut up his neck and liver, he fell to his side, heaving. and he whimpered and jolted like a starving young puppy dog.

sally had told me she couldnt come up with a definitive answer, on the shift, change, or reason at all, if any one existed–but had found some interesting unknown eventually: rich, through one late night psychedelic trip with a strange medicine substance he had bought from a strange medicine man at a bar, had turned himself on to god–or rather flicked a switch inside his brain which forced a turn to god–or whatever he wanted to believe, see, or call it. like a definitive textbook on the subject had fallen high above his bookshelf and landed open and glowing by his wrinkled toes. and it was the hidden answer and truth there in plain sight–always underneath our bedliners, floor boards, and oceans, though not always visible to the naked eye. and to understand this knowledge was addicting–according to her and her library research–and rich wanted to really know and live in it or exploit it or fix it or something. and so like a detective in the night she found the name of the meds (i forget in my retelling) the man (some kind of snake oil shaman–according to her–ive no idea), and the price: husband, father, and sweet death. though rich didnt die in this instance he was about to go to his first of many future visits to the psych ward (he would die there later on, though much after our encounter, and from an arguably different and absurder cause: choking on water and white bread) and this left sally fleeing back to hometown and the newborn with her parents for an uncertain time being–and so then she continued to question the meaning of life: her whole bus ride and walk to and through downtown. and she considered it fate that we happen to cross paths again, but knew she was heading my way anyway, even if subconsciously–

and then i missed her so. and that rush of feeling lit the soaking wet gasoline heart in my chest–a sudden poignant spark–a chain nicking the highway. fire, burned, desire, and heart. and then she asked if i was even listening, in which i replied, i think so.

and she said, okay, good, good. ive kept it from my family, my friends, my journals. i think i needed to just tell somebody already, you know? before i went wild, before i went crazy, before i felt desperate like rich.

do you think, i asked, rich possibly got high and went hunting and wandering like the old gnome in the woods because he hadnt told his story?

his story?

his ring, his tick, the reason he married, had a baby and worked and bought this and that. do you think some animal drooling with rabies foam was locked somewhere behind his heart just begging to be let go? and that weird enthusiasm, that rush and desperate need to be let loose— maybe it smelled steak, saw a plane, got lost in the garden, whatever—pushed his search out for a key from his home to sacred search of hidden anomalies?

she studied my clock face, twisting and turning, and arms waving about like wild banshee and snorting like a warthog trying to explain what i saw in her lips and broken eyes.

im not threatening you, or accusing you, i assured her. im explaining that he found the key—or so he thought he did or maybe he did, or whatever it doesnt matter—in this sacred holy substance and that he really just needed to cry? cry on the shoulder of his mother or the moon or the sun, and there was no rocking that live grenade to sleep because it was always a live grenade from the start, or tnt, red, and sparkling, and busting to explode–hell, and maybe–maybe–he did unlock that cage for that strange inner animal beast and instead of setting him free from this burden, like it was supposed to, like he thought it would since the beginning of his search, it only let out a rabid dog man that ran straight for the steak it smelt this entire time in hiding: his brain?

or, even worse, what if he did find a key, the sacred holy key, but it was not the key to the dog man wanting to escape his heart but the key to the haunted rattlesnake, resting dead, asleep, unnoticed and unbothered, and as soon as it was prodded with that key it awoke and struck like hell? like it was a whole different thing–like he sought the wrong reaction and got the wrong reaction–

like he opened a whole different can of beans?

yeah, right, exactly. he missed the point completely, and awoke hell.

his god–hell?

no, his god is his god, his god is the god. he slipped, he hiccuped, he brought a gun to the door of the devil–who was simmering, though patient–but now since he found a stranger with a gun in his front yard felt threatened so kicked down the door hisself and rushed him overnight–and now he has the truth. and now it is over.

its over, for rich, is it really? dont say it, phee! rich is dead? oh please dont say it!

or–i backtracked–or–actually–i dont know.

and i didnt say this to comfort her or sugarcoat a harsh reality. i truly didnt know. and that death statement slipped my tongue from a base of nothing. because how the hell would i know? just too many ideas at once, i guess.

i continued, no. i dont know if its over. i dont know how that story plays out and i dont know enough about things. so im sorry for frightening you.

then whats the difference, phee?

about what?

known or unknown, whats the difference? what happens with each option going forward? is there a path to follow–paths–or twisty freeways, or stairs, or i dont know any metaphors, phee! whats going on? what the hell is going on? what does one do?

i guess–i guess its really up to him–us–you–er–whomever. i guess we have to see where he takes it...i think. see how we take it. see if we even know.

oh phee! and she leaned over and hugged me and gripped me tight i coughed a frost puff and it almost brought me to tears. but i stayed held-breath and frozen, staring, when finally my eyes closed and i leaned over into her strawberry hair to comfort. she shuttered and i sighed.

then a rustic growl from behind, you guys want some coffee?

it was a funnily dressed man in slacks–high above his ankles–old tweed blazer, elbow patches and all. tiny tin glasses, and a tough collection of graying curls under a flat brown cap. after our shock, startle, and twist, i couldnt get a word out and only stared at him–sally too–with a mouth half-open, and an eyebrow high and reeling. but then, in no time, he past us to one old red door neighboring the thrift shop and unlocked it with rattling keys. he entered a closet-sized cafe in swift and sudden silence, just as he had spoken.

i rubbed sallys shoulder and spoke, you want some coffee, sally?

and there was a moment of quiet where i felt she wouldnt answer, though i was content and stared off into the street. but just as my thoughts began to boil they halted with a solemn,

sure–

that day was spent of more kicking of the rocks and scouring of the parking lots and we walked along dusty lonely freeways that led around and through orchards orange and yellow and vibrant and wet and just so wonderful i wanted to travel the world. she spoke of mexico, i spoke of france, and we both agreed on new york: man what would that be like? we never thought we would know, but the symbolic beauty of it, its cities and towers and lights and people and one dollar food–the whole lot of it, how amazing! i feared our romanticizing of such a mythical legend, time and place but she assured me that there was nothing to hold back on anything–let some stupid fear keep us from experience? sure, yeah, she was right. and i took those heavy chains off. but we stopped some time through a dirt road, the dead end of a road, and some miles from the elementary school i had gone to, seemingly only to ponder.

    this blue bird was yapping out to the mists and clouds of the day, cawing its worries and fears of another storm, of its babies, or family, or the flights they never took to florida–much warmer places–and maybe she was lonely. a single feathered mom should not be expected to travel under such dire circumstances of a storm, even if it was the best option. how could you blame them for sticking around? to the tree? what if it was the only way they knew? what if it was the only place they flew? well, i didnt know or consider any of this when i grimaced hard and halted my feet to the sharp cries of trees around us.

sally asked me, why are your eyes pinching like that? while glued to my shivering shoulder, sides, and hands deep in long pockets.

i dont know. i guess i just cant stand the caw. that birds screeching my ears off.

well she might just be excited for the cool weather now? birds cant sweat in the heat, you know.

i think shes just trying to bother us.

no, no, never, they would never do that. theyre too busy doing busy bird things. why would they bother two people on the trail? its not her trail and she knows that.

well she should caw herself back to the egg.

now, thats not fair, phee. not at all. at least shes doing it.

doing it? doing what?

yeah, doing it. at least shes out doing it. living. doing something and being well enough to sing about it all loud and proud and unabashed–even if she is taking a rest just now. just singing.

living? living. am i not living?

you act like youre living, phee–i do too, maybe–but you never know. were all so comfortable. are you living, phee?

i looked down at my muddy walking shoes. my clothes, old and tired but efficient. and the woman taming my spaz of a body while cool drafts of industrial smoke escaped my lungs like white sharp breath. and i thought i thought it through nice and well enough in that second. as well enough as i thought i could with the time given.

she repeated, are you, phee? are you living?

yeah, i said. yeah, yeah. im living.

are you trying to convince me? with sly smirk and eyebrow cocked and squinted eye.

no, no. i see living. im—im sure of it.

i see you too and i dont see living...and i see me and i dont see living either. no earthquakes in...years. just going because the going is what we chose, i guess.

now youre just messing with me, girl.

her head fell back against my shoulder, fireplace feeling, and we continued on.

whenre you gonna play another show for me, phee? she said.

then my hand came free of its pocket cell and it stroked the back of my matted hair, im not sure about a show.

her head shook ruffled feathers and she looked up at me, you not sure about a show? whats wrong with you? play a show for me, cmon phee, whatre you scared of?

no, no, im not scared—im not scared of anything—im just not sure anythings booked right now. we really do need to get back in the saddle, though. and as soon as possible. it has been a while.

oh you. how longs it been?

shit, i dont know, a month or so...

a month only, thats it?

no, im wrong. its only been a few days i think–a week, maybe?

is that still too long for you–you and your fellas?

for the things i want to do, yeah. yeah its far too long. ive been wasting time kicking rocks in parking lots and such things like that.

do you think youre wasting time with me, phee?

no, no, i dont think that, sally. im just trying to talk to myself, try to remind myself theres work to do, yknow?

and are we living, phee?

i stopped in my tracks again. and then a more echoed call came from that blue bird some ways away. and then a clearer one from a murder of crows rushing off closer to the great empty sky.

yeah, i assured the surrounding. yeah. look at us. were living. but all this questioning and all this road is starting to make me think that all this living constitutes to nothing–and that all these moments are just like all these moments and that all these moments exist in an unbothered and unmoving time. and that all these moments dont really need all that much thinking—and all these moments maybe dont really matter all that much anyway. is that good or bad? to realize that—or think that way?

i dont know.

i dont know, either.

when we looped back around the orchard and made our way back past the trail and through the untamed wet jungle mass of woods, she danced. and she made me dance with her like kids back then and blissfully unaware of the truth we were. or the divorce or the insults or the looks we all got and the urchins we all awoke skipping through all that downtown where all that music played and all those early christmas bells jingled and all those clean coat bums moaned for a dollar a toothache. and we trotted we did all the way back down to her temporary motel with hands held tight and memories faded and new ones created and my lips on her neck and my nose in her hair and her breath in my mouth and her voice in my ear. the place was a real low life addicts paradise. but its where we giggled our way through her door unlocked like giddy school children and slept in the same bed hurriedly without pants on, and closed our eyes slowly under the same covers, and laid there unabashed just like that bird and slept.

for hours—

the boring rapport of the young newsman from the tiny tv was just enough jarring static to wake me up. and with my lids heavy and falling and fighting to keep up i got a glimpse of a smooth hazel back at the end of the bed, quickly covered by a small cotton tee and heavy sweater. and my body was cold–from the icey shoulders to the frozen neck–almost shivering as if i was laying atop ice cube covers like some fresh deli lobster, completely sobering myself, intoxicated with emotion.

i moaned, its c-o-o-old, rushing and kicking and wrestling to escape under the rough, hard, and bleach-stained blankets. and sally stood up and said enthusiastically,

cmon! lets go find ourselves a show! i know theres one out there, i saw flyers and pictures and letter stamps everywhere downtown. cmon, get up, get up. lets go for old times sake! cmon, cmon–pheonix! get up!

mmm–no.

phee! get up!

with no response she ripped the covers off my body– and there was i, curled like anorexic fetus, naked and tense and bunched up together like a tiny tight ball of arachnids.

okay, okay. im gettin up, i said.

i even showered, too, in this euphoric nirvana i had– caught and toyed and fucked with like a spider snatching prey from its web: it was fantastic and i feasted.

we danced in the early evening night to that brick venue with its light patches of snow and evaporated vomit and crushed and stolen and half-empty cans like two wanderlust hitchhikers. and inside some band was playing their brand of punk rock–my brand of punk rock and your brand of punk rock and her brand of punk rock and jumping up and down and wild chewing gum visions of table top doodles, and leatherbound sketches of holy books pried and prayed open and torn against new skin for one last new look at the prophecy–and the crows were spilling out the door, all apart of the same scene. and they bobbed and jumped and danced and watching it all i felt old–real old and odd and useless. it was like this cannon ball in my chest and sinking–sinking down lower and lower and growing hotter and hotter and glowing orange and red and pink and yellow and like i had never felt this part of me before–and i swear i had just been them right there on that stage and mixed up in that crowd. and i swear i had just cut the strings clean, mean, and planted seed to do so–and confidently. then a cold sweat began as if trying to fight it off.

sally paid our way in–a few bucks at most–though still i asked,

is that alright?

to which she replied, i dont think that its any problem at all right now, and ill make back whatever in a second.

so we squeezed up against a wall where we tried to dance for a few numbers but i kept stumbling over boots and shoes and people and sally began to give me a playful questioning look until finally i grabbed her close and we studied the players and the music instead. swaying and swaying, we swayed back and forth and up against and through the ropes and all along the body of tide. and i couldnt help but feel that burning in my stomach, that intense cold that came from the paradoxical heat of the cannonball—and the feeling that made me sweat and bite my tongue and force my head against the wall for stability. the tips of my fingers hurt, the veins in my arms, and this itch that ran down my back like a snowy slide until i began to get tired. a heat and a cold with their fish hooks pierced along every division of my body and tugging and yanking and pulling until me glued down to the cement floor taking it up the middle. and an escape needed to happen. and right away—while i suffered and moaned and cried mercy and defeat all in a dozen seconds. though it was so much to take, why bubble up like this now?

and the crowd got only wilder. and pits ignited here left and right and everything was swirling so fast i felt the need to heave and leave and cry home. and sally was laughing so i smiled back at her and i felt the sun behind me, and a hand on my shoulder, just breathing ever so slightly against the light hairs on my neck and whispering strange analogies in another modern language at my back–just then the music started sounding like two howling dogs to an ambulance crying by and then soon like the bubbling wails of a falling brick building all unbothered and all untouched and all unassuming to man. like to cross an intersection buzzing with rush hour traffic and to come home happily just to smile at the milkman. all the while my melting windows howled from their two stories above, tortured by that spinning daze.

and the question–cold–that brought up into my mind was one that stung and stayed and bounced around. against the musty cell walls of my brain and through the pink crumpled tissue of my struggle and strain, repeating, repeating, repeating: am i living? am i living? am i lingering? and then: are they living? what are they doing? are they doing it? so what is the problem? at one time i would have screamed for an encore, jumped up on stage and begged to lead their group, now i stare obliviously, sacredly, and off-put like an invader, outsider, or scientist looking in and wondering why and i was scared. im like the old man with the dirty beard and set. i am not naive to this sweaty presence and it is all too familiar. i am not the student with his toes stuck through the door and wanting and pushing his way in. and i am not their parent or authority figure with clipboard and pen—no statues in my name and goodies left to gift out. but i dont feel the nostalgia i should feel, the grip or ache that questioned the straight and narrow—and was this heartbreaking? was this growing up? was this always a part of the path? would did john lennon do? what would he do? do my lawyers have to get involved? is this the war waging on? is this the forever war or are all the years behind me fighting racking up to something? anything substantial? the devil on my right shoulder or the angel on my left speaking truths i am too full to understand? is that gun at my back getting its hammer cocked by my own left thumb just by sitting? i dont understand it. is this not supposed to be it? is it this? an eternal fight? i wanted to drop dead. but was too shaky to do so.

i tapped on sallys shoulder but she didnt move so i poked it a few times harder until halfway through the song i shouted in her ear, i gotta go! im gonna go!—hit the john!

okay! she said back and kissed me—sharp, fast, and indulgent—i loved her—something was wrong and i bursted—

i rushed out of there, plowing through many soaking bodies, until i reached the front doors to fresh, biting air and tumbled through the little crowd toward great empty streets where a light snow had began to fall and melt and steam across the whole carcass of my skin. my steps matched the palpitations of my heart and i jerked and convoluted, dodging bums and street corners and flickering lights. at one point i passed an old tree whose roots had uprooted the sidewalk and left one giant concrete square atop another facing me. so it caught my already dilapidated failing right shoe and tore the rest of the sole off until my dirt-brown sock fell through and i felt the cool of the road against my toes.

before i came across the new blinding gas station lights at the end of town, my entire sock was soaking water and getting damper with each step–i couldnt see it, everything was black. clenching myself tight, i pulsed violent shivers that yanked me this way and that until i tripped over a high curb and landed before the propane refill station at the start of the lot. on the ground i took off what was left of my soleless shoe and then the other one after a second of thought so the juxtaposition wouldnt disrupt my pace. this left both of my feet even but wet. and now the almost invisible snow fell with a light freezing rain–i couldnt see it, everything was black. i sneezed myself upright and continued on like a wounded zombie until i reached the side of the mini-mart where then my eyes closed automatically–the instant action of a reaction that reached them dry and red and puffy. they closed hard, they felt tense.

slowly, my body straining in jittery flex, i curled from my stomach. my hands jolted to my hair and pulled at them in fists shaking with agitation. teeth gritted, and coming, still slowly, to one knee, feeling the deathly urge to scream and shout and kill the innards that left my body fighting for a fix and fighting for a solution. it was unknown to me, it was unknown to him, and every instinct reacted at once. i fell back to my bum and tears welted underneath and around spasming eyelids but they were light enough to wobble still and so lingered impatiently. this was it. the whirlwind of my life around me and surrounding me and throwing things at me i forgot or never realized or forgot i never realized or taking control like the black storm cloud it did to my plains. my mind was blank but my feelings were there. my head was bleak but i knowed it, the war had started at the gunshot and raced on ahead over my intuition. my actions acted on a notion that seemed so primitive, so alien, and so insignificant, that it frustrates me so. to a point of ripping out and off my skin to let the steam go and let loose and burst away awry! the man had shot me down under the covers but i knew it was happening. i had been seduced by a pretty idea that pretty ideas could stay pretty for years and years without a watering of the bricks. without a paving of the flowers or patting of the dog. i could keep my baked goods out of the fridge and under the freezer until after christmas time where i could go back and mmm so delicious start munching on them yum yum yum yum. but now the dust settled with my face in the gruff palm of this ancient idea. a treasure lost and found and lost again–out and forever.

my hand shot down on this paved white road, the other broke skin and the knuckles punching rocks for a few answers before trying to get a grip on the smooth cement and scraping nails and getting chills. all a solution, finding the solution. me at the center of this event: i bit my thumb, i tugged my ears, i scratched my arms, i flexed my legs, i curled my toes, i grunted and moaned, i twisted my neck, i cut my fingers, i ripped off my skin, i squeezed myself, i scratched my back to blood, i choked my neck, i shook my head, i twisted and contorted, i bit my tongue, and i hit my eyes–so hard, they squeaked. i was searching for a hidden button, an idea, or trigger. hidden beneath timeless symbols and witchcraft, the odd, timeless signs and languages undiscovered and untranscribed for years–things that were never the same after this event or that–i dont understand it. if i swallowed a rock and pretended it was my life, would i just be sulking in this great womb of sadness?

there was supposed to be a green that would mean the end of this life and the restart of another–my madness and journey and career and ever-so-calculated soul because there had to be. the end all to the ultimate weapon and the ultimate weapon. but i couldnt find it on my body. and i could only realize the shift and the change. and so i could only freak at the thought. so i sat.

i was too tired. i brought up my knees to my elbows and buried my face in the sanctity of my personal void. and wanted to shout but didnt shout and wanted to bite my fingers off but didnt bite my fingers off and wanted to pull my eyes lower, lower, lower, as low as they could get and write more letters to god and have sudden impulse faith and buy into all those kinds of words from the rich lab coat people but none of that stood on three legs. none of it. nothing ever did. so then the fourth leg would have to be something. something else, right?

i stayed steady, still, and my mind halted with race car breaks til my heart came to a sharp stop–then silence. bugs whizzing around, lights whining around, cars screeching and racing miles away, carts topped with luggage and clothes and bundled in tarp being dragged by struggling wheels, flappy stomps of trashcan shoes, and the tense piercing whistle that comes from the rush to silence. squeaky cart. nothing, nothing, nothing. think of nothing and get a grip. feel nothing and find your balance. melt into the floor and die unknowledgeable. there was nothing to be known.

–and then her moments kiss–true love disguised as a fling–the only thing it could be–or would ever be–a fling–

and then i finally cracked and tears fell like rolling gutters in the fall. but only for a moment.

and then nothing—

when i awoke the next morning, back in the bed, stained with sweat and grief and looking more and more like the raccoons home or bears breakfast, i could not face the white morning sun. and i expected nothing of my blinds no longer, and i had to teach myself to become apathetic to that light, and force myself through habit—it was a fact that everytime my lids were irritated and became bothered id pinch my ass cheek or punch my ribs. this was a formal act of something, i was sure of it. and i stayed in a dreamlike state much after i was awake and staring at the muddled dots of my ceiling. and i could feel my brain, groggy, moving back and forth the motion of a lava lamp, or some kind of air mass of radio waves circulating in and out an unexplainably soft way. thatd kept the mind mostly blank, but could not stop the stomach from continuing its turning, still.

a real hunger came over me—for real, real food—a sickening hunger, one painful and tearing and distracting, and hard to tell if it was real. so i strapped myself to the frame, bedsheet handcuffs and gagged my mouth with socks and waited my pain away, and this struggle lasted a few hours, a healthy answer to an unfair obsession, if any at all—the attention to detail caught mimis call—i couldnt hide from mimi. she knocked but came in just as fast. stumbling over boxers and stacks of paper and general trash, she asked if id been out practicing again, and if the drums had been played and that she had heard them and such. and i told her i slept with sally. so she gave me a huff and a puff and retreated out the hall and down the stairs trepidly. and thinking i was still doing the right thing i shuffled my defrosting limbs to the desk where i studied my fallen toys and asked them bogus questions focused on their subtle features and small feet. til noon called with a country cooking smell and it stopped me mid sentence—and that smell was demanding and i could not fight it no longer so i rushed out of my cellar in an instant and was crawling to the kitchen in a second watching mimi rest a decorated white bird atop the oven exuding—an early thanksgiving supper.

hungry?

yes. and it made me want to cry—surprisingly—that little bit. and i couldnt find a reason why.

we ate in silence, stifled and unnerving. there were a thousand questions that needed asking and a thousand answers that needed answering. from mimi and myself. and i could go at it alone. she would just have to realize that—through no words at all—and i felt her stare—her long chewing movements as she focused on my face dragging down.

and in the middle of my mashed potato mouth feast there was a knock at the door. then the overlapping triplet mess of two–then a few hard ones–all in a very impatient second. mimi rose to her feet but id put my fork down first and stood up, motioning her back. i got it.

without a second thought, i swung that door open and was instantly shadowed by the bust of two giant chests. big stinky metal looking fellas. they were the taxi drivers of my trip back to odessa from frisco–jacks friends.

hey, i said. you are dennis. and you are darby. i remember.

hey, the bearded one, a waving shirt with fading cheap graphic, spoke first.

then the second, more complete with a browned and fraying black hoodie, jumped first, wheres our money?

huh?

wheres my money?

did you line jack?

did we line, jack? you were gonna pay us! we didnt take no jack home!

and he showed me a knife. a cheap, long knife, with a shiny metal blade and tiny plastic grip. and it glittered in the sunlight like an angel.

a knife?

yes-its-a-fucking-knife!

why? please, cmon now.

why? for my fifty bucks you fucking dope! git me my fifty bucks!

i shook. and i thought i was playing it cool. but then i blanked. and with a cold sweat running down my arms and neck i asked,

who are you guys?

you think youre fucking funny? playing games like that? you just said–he raised the blade to my face, eyes darted to the point, mouth half open, fear rolling off my tongue–maybe seriously this time–and i asked, how did you find me?

and he just shook his head in a twitch of discomfort–back-glancing his partner–fingers sweating and readjusting the dripping handle. no more words from him except disgruntled huffs and puffs, similar to aunt mimis. his partner behind a fat frozen statue, staring off into home except really looking at nothing in particular. swaying slightly with the sharp and cold breeze that reckoned more snow. and i dont remember which one was dennis and which one was darby.

coming back, standing straight, crossing arms, i aint got the fifty bucks, i said. i aint got the fifty bucks, but i promised you id get the fifty bucks.

thats right. thats right you said youd get the fifty bucks—and we were promised the fifty bucks, so we want the fifty bucks right god damn now! aint no time for no funny business, aint no time for none of that funny shit. give us our fifty bucks. or—or ill kill ya.

behind, a clacking of silverware halted—mimi trying to listen in—i stepped outside, closing the door. i thought id felt nothing but i was scared. i tried to mask it off as stoicism but the apathy was frightening too. and no one fell for it anyway.

i aint got your money, i said. i aint got no money.

and then dennis or darby (the one with the knife) leaned stiffly to his side and shook his head slightly—looked like a red balloon about to explode. the knife shrunk like the pulling back of a spring. a wave of white heat swept across me like the spilling of a bucket of hot fear and gliding along my organs fluidly in one motion. then my eyes went back to him.

no money, i said.

and his trap released and i jumped to the side and getting slashed briefly and struck him in the blocky glasses i did with a birdy chirp of a grunt. and as those stone frames flew off a wild spinning top, the other hobbled over—dennis or darby (the one without the knife)—and swung his heavy arm a baseball bat knocking my neck back and throwing me against the door–bash–and damn i didnt like that. with my eyes closed and my tears running i threw freely as a blind man, where i hit nothing and broke nothing and cut wind and felt the sharp, slippery blade of something enter my abdomen and release–like a flu shot in and out in a flash. it oozed warmth around my shirt and searing hot inside my shirt and eyes opened wide. in a blurring, wet frantic i could make out the shapes of two giant monster blobs before i felt another flu shot right at my chest and i fell stiff from shock and pain, curling my favorite fetal position without a word. shaking like a dog.

i felt everything. but saw nothing at all. my pockets were rummaged through, there was sluggish chattering, i was tossed this way and that without empathy and left sprawled out at the bottom of the wooden stairs robbed of nothing because i had nothing–and instead of checking inside they scattered off at mimis call, where they would tumble down the sidewalk, into their beater and scream off into the broad daylight with abrupt feeling of justice served. dennis and darby. where the smaller of the two called the driver den-den. and i think they were on drugs.

i lay there motionless and feeling sorry for myself again and very, very sleepy. and as time faded with my blackening eyes, i heard the screech of my dear aunt, who loved me more than i could ever realize–

the hospital was no place for a growing boy—except i was no boy anymore and everyone started correctly guessing my age (where in they used to think i was a lot older than i really was in highschool). they often said i looked like i was in my twenties and they were often right nowadays. a twenty something being wheeled off through the halls of an old er. with banners on the windows proclaiming its excellence—only in the last coupla years. what a wild dream.

i thought i was dead. but heard the nurses, men and women, speak with their confident young voices and bickered back and forth through an anxious frenzy. muffled through their masks i couldnt make out complete anecdotes—he-said, she-saids—but smiled at their wit and charm anyway. i was feeling in a sitcom, where i could fall asleep on the lazy sunday couch to the sound of automatic laughter.

and this moment lasted until i blinked again—one too many times—and found id been sleeping too much again, drool on the bed and blanket, and that time had passed by in an instant again—and of course never to be brought back again. where once i saw blinding white hospital lights, i now saw the strange cluttered bumps of the top of my ceiling, where my fan swayed back and forth and still looked like it was about to free from its hinges and kill me. it was so cold, what air was it even circulating? hot air? hot air gone with the season and left behind in little jean jackets that dont fit no more. kept long after expiration because of how much you cared for them so–and we were dropped in the bitter antarctic in shorts and lollipop and umbrella cap–or maybe i crawled there myself, dressed up there myself, thinking i smelled pie, but only found shit pie instead, and threw a baby fit, staying motionless. could be. i dont know.

PART 3:
THE INS AND OUTS AND GALLOPS OF TIME!

the talk with the doctors was short and sweet, from what i remember, and i dont remember much at all—

they really didnt know what to say when you told them that, mimi told me.

and what did i say, i dont remember.

you basically told them you were—something went off in the kitchen and she said to hold on and rushed down the stairs, never to be seen again. she left her brand new christmas oven mitts on my bed, where i layed stiff like wood plank, thick bandages weighing me down. i felt like a brick and was thirsty like a tick and began to smack my lips. when i started moving the blankets around, through my soreness and discomfort, i thought id write jack and let him know i was off for a second—while i recovered—because i hate to leave him hanging anymore than i had. but the pain kept me from going farther than an inch. so that would have to wait, for now, unfortunately.

there was a postcard on my nightstand, next to a glass of water. big balloons of hospital animals half-deflated, cards and little gift bags—all just noticed—and my old dog leash hidden across the way by unfolded laundry on my desk.

i was aiming for the water and gripped it with malnourished anger and, trembling like the hood of an old car, dropped the heavy glass—straw and all—on the wooden planks of my floor. the postcard bounced down with it and it landed on its back side. i could only make out the giant blocky letters and frowny face at the corner: SORRY, JACK.

sorry jack? i strained for it, wet and floppy, the ink smearing. it read:

I DONT KNOW THE RIGHT WAY TO SAY THIS SO IM JUST GONNA SAY IT PLAIN. I FEEL LIKE IVE TRIED MY BEST WITH YOU AND YOU HAVENT BEEN COOPERATING LIKE YOU SHOULD HAVE. SINCE THE BEGINNING. YOUVE LET ME DOWN MORE TIMES THAN ONE WITH YOUR TROTTING ALONG. FRANKLY, I AM SICK OF IT, I AM FED UP WITH IT. I FOUND SOME PEOPLE DOWN HERE. MULTIPLE DRUMMERS AND EVEN SINGERS WHO ARE MOTIVATED AND MORE THAN HAPPY TO GET THE BALL ROLLING— AND KEEP IT ROLLING. SORRY IT HAD

TO HAPPEN THIS WAY BUT NOW YOU CAN REST LIKE YOU ALWAYS WANTED. SORRY, JACK.

okay. and i let it fall. okay. and all that work–nevermind. okay.

hey mimi! i called hoarse and phlegmmy, mimi!

uh, uh, what!? an echo from down the hall with the heavy shut of the oven and the clinky slam of some smaller trinkets.

mimi, im thirsty, can i get a water?

what? a water? sure! sure thing! ill be right up!

and in the blink of an eye my door cracked open and a huge mug of water, ice, straw and all, was lowered to me. i rested the glass up to my neck bandage and sipped from the straw like a big-eyed baby. quick bursts and quicker breaks to take quick breaths.

mimi stared, innocently, arms clasped upon her colorful, christmas apron.

hows recovery? she asked.

recovery? i thought. recovery? is this recovery? am i healing or just resting–this isnt needless i know that, im injured physically, im hurting, and even if i wanted i couldnt play or get up or work. no, no, no i am injured. but why why does this have to stop me? why cant i run on forever, think and believe forever? i dont know. i believed—im sure of it—just unsure of what exactly to. a believer of something, i dont know, someone? what a tricky word: belief. i cant even say it without sounding silly, and i thought i was serious. i needed to heal. i know i needed to. there was no way around that. but something, something urged me. i was wasting time, i was wasting precious time and being lazy. and the sooner i got up and got on the phone or wrote to jack or to someone to let them know: hey, hey, i dont want to be here, i swear, i dont even want to be here but god herself stuck me down here and struck me with a backhand for making empty promises—that werent empty to me, i truly believed—and so dont get mad at me, for i am already mad at myself, please, please, please, i would work if i could, i would i would i would i sweat, leave me alone! dont leave me alone, i need it, i need it, i need the pulsing to be working! i need it, i need it i need it! dont let me go, jack, sally, friends, family, strangers, debt collectors, dont let me go! give me a second ill be back ill be back i know i will, believe me, believe in something. believe me when i tell ya ill get back faster, faster, faster, i just need to rest, i need to because i have to—you know that i know i would rather be in the river running, hammering down nails on the infinite beam or post, chalkboards with complicated but necessary solutions. you know it. believe in that. have faith and believe in me—

phoenix? hows recovery?

what? me? recovery? oh its fine, its fine—hey, can you get me that envelope on my desk and a pen and paper i have to—

no. she said calmly, sternly, affectionately. no, no, none of that. you need to rest.

rest yeah, sure, im resting, but i can still work while im here. i can. i need to prove it. i fucked up. i fucked up big time. i dont want to be useless, laying around here like some bum, doing nothing, being nothing.

no, phoenix, she said again. you need to rest. no one needs to hear anything right now, no one needs to see anything right now, you need to rest for yourself. just for yourself

you dont understand, mi!

yes i do. let it go.

let it go? let it go? ive been at it for years! i was there since the beginning, i was doing it, i was on the show, on a roll, i was there! let it go? what do you mean let it go? i cant its my life!

i know you were there, phoenix. but he wasnt. so let it go.

he thinks i gave up! and i gave up! i want back in! i need him to know!

you never gave up. you needed to rest. and you need to rest now—still.

but i dont want to rest.

thats why youre half-dead, boy. take it as a sign. the warm will-a-god. divine hands and timing. take it as a sign that youre beat and that you need a rest.

impatient and growing in discomfort, i thought id just rip myself out of this lazy bed and get to it myself, then, myself, myself, yeah. i dont need no shouting match, i just need to get up. i need to get moving. i need to push through this hunger-strike. and as i began squirming around, a soft, bony hand rested on my shoulder and gently lowered me back down. and in an even more gentler tone,

phee, no. its time to rest.

and i looked up at her, intense, boiling fire in my eyes, and face stone with angry, sharp curves that made for a warrier's wooden mask. my head fell back in my pillow, looking at the ceiling, and i felt the pains of my knife wounds, and my headache, and my hunger, and my cold knees. i wanted to fight but i couldnt fight and i realized that under it all when i awoke and it was almost like falling through faint clouds of dust, my body settling on the hard packed orange dirt, in natural silence. nothing and no one around me. just me in my sunglasses and coat staring at pale blue sky. and i lost nothing to nobody. and i felt calm. who is she, that god? what is she speaking, and why is it in twisted tongues?

oh, but isnt it obvious? why must you seek for answers devoid of sense, boy? why had this long-enough slumber caused you so much harm? what does birds life song mean to me? the sun or rain when pressed against my cracking alligator skin? mist in the soft kisses of forbidden lost nights long ago and pressing forward and shooting bullets? my life on the leash. has my life been an isolated angle? a deadly dose poisoning day by day, thought by thought, second by second? who am i speaking to on the moonlit docks shadow, silhouetted by passing children and buses and jumbo jet planes? and where does one boy stand against the ruckus of it all running by?

mi, i dont understand it.

what is there to understand? you just gotta handle it.

i turned to her, i just gotta handle it? what do i do to handle it?

you eat.

i eat?

yes. you eat.

eat. but what do i eat?

ill go fix you something. im sure you wont move by the time i get back?

um—yes, i said. the urge had left me like the night. reluctantly and impatiently, i let it go, it let itself go. all in another blink. she got up and got going.

and down the stairs i could hear the whiney chime of the phone ring, the commotion of the pick-up, and the slam-ring of it ending. the dog barked a happy bark and i smelled his golden fur from my room and closed my eyes to sigh.

staring at the wall, darting back and forth the patterns and spider webs. my body hurt and my mind was lost, not wandering. then i closed my eyes and fell into a dreamless and endless sleep. the fourth leg had to be me.

so then today

i would start

with sleep.

www.ingramcontent.com/pod-product-compliance
Lightning Source LLC
LaVergne TN
LVHW092051060526
838201LV00047B/1345